THE GREEKS

Susan Peach
Anne Millard
BA, Dip. Ed., Dip. Arch., Ph.D.

History consultant: **Graham Tingay** MA

Edited by **Jane Chisholm**

Designed by **Robert Walster, Radhi Parekh** and **Iain Ashman**

Illustrated by **Ian Jackson**

Additional illustrations by
Richard Draper, Robert Walster, Gerry Wood, Peter Dennis, Nigel Wright and **Gillian Hurry**

With thanks to **Anthony Marks**

Contents

How to use this book

Dates

Most of the dates in this book are from the period before the birth of Christ. These dates are shown by the letters BC, which stand for "Before Christ". Dates in the period after the birth of Christ are indicated by the letters AD, which stand for Anno Domini, meaning "Year of the Lord".

Dates in the BC period are counted backwards from the birth of Christ. The main centuries are .

1-99BC	= first century BC
100-199BC	= second century BC
200-299BC	= third century BC
300-399BC	= fourth century BC
400-499BC	= fifth century BC
500-599BC	= sixth century BC
600-699BC	= seventh century BC

Experts have not been able to discover exact dates for many events in Greek history, and most archaeological finds can only be dated imprecisely. In this book, where a date is only approximate, it is preceded by the abbreviation "c.". This stands for *circa,* which is the Latin word for "about".

Periods of Ancient Greek history

Experts divide Ancient Greek history into several approximate periods, which are shown on the chart below. These periods have been used throughout this book.

c.2900-1000BC	= The Bronze Age
c.1100-800BC	= The Dark Ages
c.800-500BC	= The Archaic Period
c.500-336BC	= The Classical Period
c.336-30BC	= The Hellenistic Period

How we know about the Greeks

Although the Ancient Greeks lived about three thousand years ago, we know a lot about how they lived. Our information comes from a variety of sources, which are shown here.

Archaeologists have dug up many Ancient Greek objects and buildings. Important sites have been excavated in Greece and in the places that the Greeks colonized. Marine archaeologists have found the wrecks of several Ancient Greek ships, some with their cargoes preserved. Greek objects have also been found in countries where they were taken by traders. For example, Minoan pots made on Crete have been dug up in Egyptian tombs (see page 5).

Archaeologists at work on a site.

Pots are some of the most useful archaeological discoveries. The Greeks decorated many of their pots with pictures of everyday life. These scenes have given experts much information about what

the Greeks looked like, what they wore, what their homes and furniture were like, and the kind of lives they lived. Many scenes in this book are based on pictures found on vases.

This vase shows potters at work.

When the Romans occupied Greece in the second century BC, they were fascinated by the buildings, statues and paintings that they discovered there. They were so impressed by Greek art that they made copies of many statues and paintings. A large number of these Roman copies have survived, although the originals have been lost.

This discus thrower is a Roman copy of a Greek statue. The Greek original has been lost.

The Greeks wrote on scrolls made out of a plant called papyrus. This rots easily, so very few original manuscripts have been found. However Greek writings have survived because people from Roman times onwards made copies of them. The copies include works by many Greek writers about history, philosophy and politics, as well as plays and poems. Coins, clay tablets and inscriptions on monuments and buildings provide other written evidence.

Part of an inscription from the wall of a Greek temple.

Silver coin from Athens.

Fragment of Greek papyrus found in Egypt.

Key dates

On some pages of this book there are charts which summarize the events of the particular period or place. There is also a chart on pages 88-89 which lists all the events in the book.

Unfamiliar words

Greek words, such as *tholos*, are written in italic type. Words that are followed by a dagger symbol, such as democracy†, are explained in the glossary on pages 90-91. If a person's name is followed by this symbol, it means that you can read more about them in the "Who's Who" on pages 85-87.

Places

There are small maps on many pages, to show where events took place. Towns or cities are marked with dots, and battles are shown with crosses.

Many places now have different names from their Ancient Greek names. In most cases the ancient names have been used, and the area is made clear by the map. The area now called Turkey is referred to throughout the book as Asia Minor, which was its name in ancient times.

Reference

At the back of this section of the book there is an appendix. This contains a detailed map of Greece, summaries of important Greek myths and legends, a section that explains who was who in Ancient Greece, a chart of the important dates in Ancient Greek history, and a glossary of Greek and other unfamiliar words.

The first Greeks

The area now called Greece consists of a land-mass on the north-eastern edge of the Mediterranean Sea and the surrounding islands.

Map of Greece

The first inhabitants arrived in Greece about 40,000 years ago. They lived in caves and hunted and gathered food. Some time before 6000BC, farming was introduced by new groups of people from the east who settled in eastern Greece.

The first farmers grew vegetables and cereal crops and kept sheep.

Around 3000BC, people in Greece discovered how to mix copper and tin to make bronze. They used it to make tools and weapons. These were harder and sharper than previous ones, which had been made of bone or flint. The improved equipment made farming and building easier. The period from 3000-1100BC is known as the Bronze Age†.

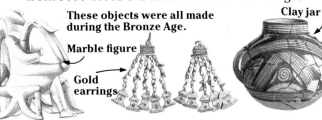

These objects were all made during the Bronze Age.

Marble figure

Gold earrings

Clay jar

As farming became more efficient, many farmers had a surplus of produce which could be exchanged for goods. Some people made a living as craftsmen by selling their goods instead of growing food. Trade made people more prosperous, the population increased and some villages grew into towns.

Farm produce could be exchanged for goods such as tools, jewellery or pottery.

From 2600-2000BC the people of the Cyclades were particularly prosperous. Craftsmen produced fine goods and there was much trade between the islands. However, the Cyclades were too small to develop further and it was on the island of Crete that the first great European civilization began.

Crete

Early Crete

The first inhabitants of Crete seem to have been farmers who settled there in about 6000BC. By about 2000BC there was a flourishing civilization on the island, with a highly organized economy and system of trade, based around a number of large palaces. There were skilled craftsmen and artists, and some people could read and write.

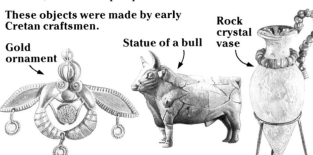

These objects were made by early Cretan craftsmen.

Gold ornament

Statue of a bull

Rock crystal vase

We know about this early civilization from archaeological evidence found on Crete. The first and most important discoveries were made by an Englishman called Sir Arthur Evans. In AD1894 he began excavating a palace at Knossos (see map above). Evans named the civilization Minoan†, after a legendary Cretan king called Minos.

The legend of Minos

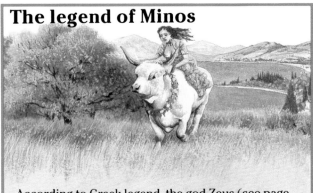

According to Greek legend, the god Zeus (see page 64) fell in love with a beautiful princess called Europa. He assumed the shape of a bull and swam to Crete with her on his back. She had three sons, Minos, Sarpedon and Rhadamanthys. Minos became the king of Crete, and his palace was at Knossos.

Although the legend says that Minos was the name of one king, experts now think that Minos may actually have been a title, like the Egyptian word Pharaoh. All Cretan kings may therefore have been known as Minos.

Life in Minoan Crete

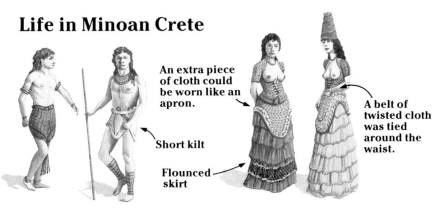

An extra piece of cloth could be worn like an apron.

Short kilt

Flounced skirt

A belt of twisted cloth was tied around the waist.

We know what the Minoans wore because their clothes were shown on many wall paintings. Men usually wore a loincloth and a short kilt made of wool or linen.

Women wore elaborate, brightly coloured dresses with tight bodices which left their breasts bare. The skirts were generally flounced.

Most people made their living from farming. They kept animals and grew crops such as wheat, barley, olives and grapes. Fishing and hunting provided extra food. This Minoan wall painting shows a young fisherman.

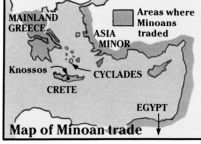

Map of Minoan trade

Areas where Minoans traded

MAINLAND GREECE

ASIA MINOR

Knossos

CYCLADES

CRETE

EGYPT

The Minoans travelled widely, both on Crete and abroad. They used carts drawn by oxen or donkeys, but as there were few roads, people often travelled by sea.

The Greek historian Thucydides says that King Minos had a large fleet of ships, which controlled the seas. This wall painting shows a variety of Minoan ships.

The Minoans traded with many foreign countries. Their pots and other goods have been found in Greece and the Cyclades and all round the eastern Mediterranean (see map).

Writing

When the Minoans started to store and export goods, they developed a system of writing to help them keep accurate records. Their first script, which was used from c.2000BC, was a form of hieroglyphic (picture) writing. In about 1900BC they introduced a second script, which we call Linear A†. As yet no-one has been able to decipher either of these scripts.

Part of a Linear A tablet

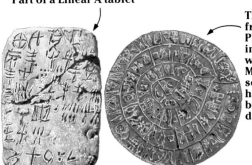

This disc, from Phaestos, is inscribed with a third Minoan script, which has not yet been deciphered.

Pottery

Minoan pots

Before the discovery of Knossos, Minoan pots had been found in Egypt. These pots had already been approximately dated, as experts had been able to establish dates for Egyptian sites. When archaeologists found a particular style of pot on Crete, they could date it by comparing it with the dated pots found in Egypt. This also meant that they could give a rough date to the Cretan site at which the pot had been discovered.

The Minoan palaces

The Minoans† often built their towns by the coast, in places where it was easy to reach the sea and the fertile farmlands. Each of the larger towns was based around a palace. The first palaces were built shortly after 2000BC and were destroyed by earthquakes about 300 years later. Little remains of these early buildings because the Minoans quickly built new, even grander palaces over the old ones. Four of these later palaces have been found, at Knossos, Zakro, Phaestos and Mallia. There is also a large villa at Hagia Triada and a few smaller sites, mostly to the east of the island.

The palace at Knossos

The largest palace was at a place called Knossos. It was built and rebuilt several times between about 1900BC and 1450BC. This picture shows how it probably looked at its height, when it covered around 20,000 square metres (215,000 square feet). Experts think that over 30,000 people lived in the palace and surrounding area.

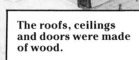
The palace was decorated with images of a bull's horns.

The roofs, ceilings and doors were made of wood.

The queen's bathroom

Knossos had an excellent water supply and drainage system. To prevent floods the heavy spring and autumn rains were channelled into gutters. The water was stored in tanks, then passed into the palace along clay pipes. The system served several toilets and bathrooms. This reconstruction shows the queen's bathroom.

The royal apartments

Each palace had private apartments set aside for the royal family. The royal apartments had large, airy rooms, decorated with colourful wall paintings known as frescoes. These were made by applying paint to wet plaster. The frescoes at Knossos have given archaeologists much valuable information about Minoan dress and customs. Most of the frescoes which can now be seen in the palace are modern reconstructions, based on fragments of the original pictures.

This fresco shows a young man wearing an elaborate headdress which suggests that he was a prince or a king.

Many paintings depict the beauty of nature. This is part of a fresco from the queen's apartment, which shows a school of dolphins.

Lighting

Light was let into the building through open shafts which ran from the roof to the ground floor. These are known as light wells. Staircases and corridors led from the light wells to the rooms on each level.

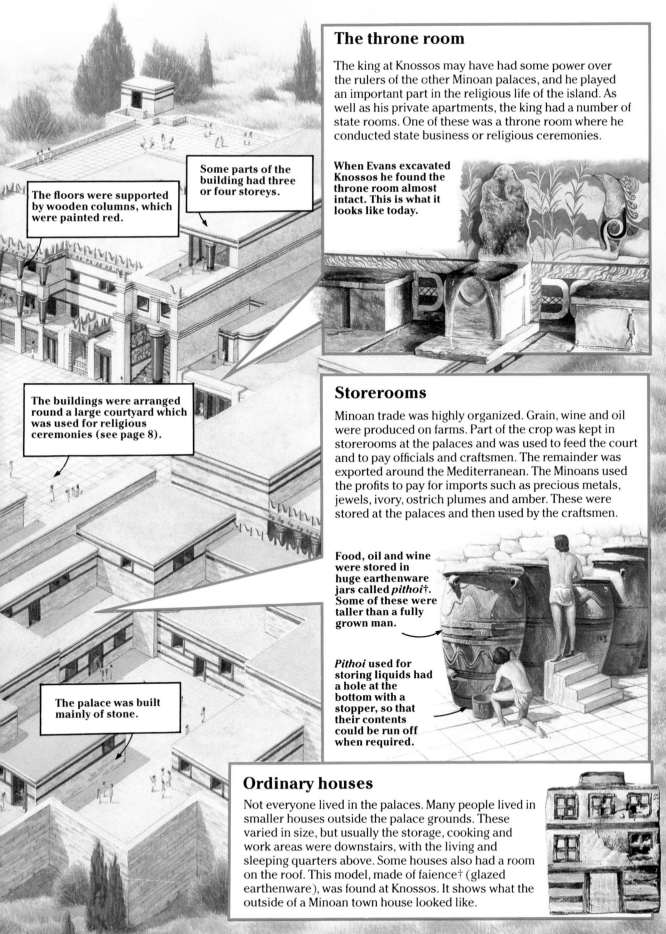

The throne room

The king at Knossos may have had some power over the rulers of the other Minoan palaces, and he played an important part in the religious life of the island. As well as his private apartments, the king had a number of state rooms. One of these was a throne room where he conducted state business or religious ceremonies.

When Evans excavated Knossos he found the throne room almost intact. This is what it looks like today.

Some parts of the building had three or four storeys.

The floors were supported by wooden columns, which were painted red.

The buildings were arranged round a large courtyard which was used for religious ceremonies (see page 8).

The palace was built mainly of stone.

Storerooms

Minoan trade was highly organized. Grain, wine and oil were produced on farms. Part of the crop was kept in storerooms at the palaces and was used to feed the court and to pay officials and craftsmen. The remainder was exported around the Mediterranean. The Minoans used the profits to pay for imports such as precious metals, jewels, ivory, ostrich plumes and amber. These were stored at the palaces and then used by the craftsmen.

Food, oil and wine were stored in huge earthenware jars called *pithoi*†. Some of these were taller than a fully grown man.

Pithoi used for storing liquids had a hole at the bottom with a stopper, so that their contents could be run off when required.

Ordinary houses

Not everyone lived in the palaces. Many people lived in smaller houses outside the palace grounds. These varied in size, but usually the storage, cooking and work areas were downstairs, with the living and sleeping quarters above. Some houses also had a room on the roof. This model, made of faience† (glazed earthenware), was found at Knossos. It shows what the outside of a Minoan town house looked like.

Minoan religion

Special rooms were set aside for religious ceremonies in Minoan palaces. Outdoor shrines were also used. Archaeological remains have revealed how the Minoans worshipped and the roles of some of their gods. It seems that goddesses were probably more important than gods, as they are much more prominent in statues and paintings. Some of them are shown here.

◄ The goddess on this seal is known as the Mistress of the Animals. She is shown on a mountain top, surrounded by animals. A young male god is worshipping her.

The Minoans ► worshipped a goddess who protected the household. She is often depicted with snakes, which were a sacred symbol.

This seal shows another important ▲ goddess who looked after crops. She is often depicted by a sacred tree and is sometimes accompanied by a young god.

Sacred symbols

The Minoans had two sacred symbols which they used to decorate palaces, tombs and pots. The bull was thought to be sacred and images of its horns were found throughout Knossos. Another common symbol was the double-headed axe, or *labrys*†.

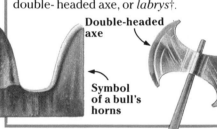

Double-headed axe

Symbol of a bull's horns

Religious ceremonies

This reconstruction shows what might have happened at a religious ceremony. Special priests and priestesses would have led the ceremony. Archaeological remains show that the Minoans made offerings of food, statues and axes to their gods.

Musicians

During the ceremony, a *libation*† (an offering of milk, wine or blood) was poured on to an altar

Sacred symbols and statues of gods

Altar

Offerings

Bull-leaping

This fresco† shows part of the bull-leaping ritual. The figure on the right was there to catch the leaper.

One of the strangest Minoan practices was bull-leaping. It seems that teams of young men and women approached a charging bull. One after the other they grasped its horns, leaped on to its back, and then to the ground. Many experts believe that this was a religious ritual, as the bull was a sacred animal. The ceremony may have taken place in the palace courtyard.

Death and the afterlife

The Minoans believed in some form of life after death. They buried dead people with food and personal possessions which they thought would be of use in the afterlife. Early tombs, dating from about 2800BC, were round stone structures which were used for many burials. Later the Minoans used individual coffins.

This coffin, found at the villa of Hagia Triada, was made in about 1400BC. It is decorated with a funeral scene showing people making offerings.

The end of the Minoans

In about 1450BC all the palaces on Crete were destroyed. Many experts have linked this event to a volcanic eruption on the island of Thera, about 110km (70 miles) north of Crete. The explosions were so violent that most of Thera was blasted away, leaving only the small crescent-shaped island now called Santorini. On Crete, this may have caused tidal waves, earth tremors, flooding and destruction of crops. Recent geological evidence suggests that the eruption may have taken place about 200 years earlier, so Minoan dates may have to be revised.

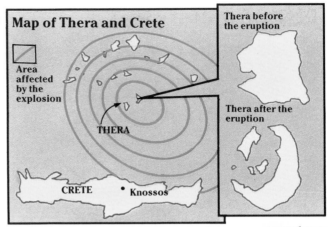

Map of Thera and Crete

Area affected by the explosion

THERA

CRETE • Knossos

Thera before the eruption

Thera after the eruption

The arrival of the Mycenaeans

Natural disasters may not have been the only cause of the Minoans' downfall. According to legend, King Minos travelled to Sicily, where he was murdered by a local king and his fleet was destroyed. This may be partly true. Perhaps there was an unsuccessful expedition to Sicily, which left Crete without a fleet. We know that by about 1450BC Crete had been invaded by a people from mainland Greece, known as the Mycenaeans.

The Mycenaeans repaired and rebuilt the palace at Knossos and became the new rulers of the island.

Around 1400BC the palace at Knossos burned down and was abandoned.

About 50 years later Knossos was destroyed again. We do not know why this happened. Perhaps the Mycenaeans fought among themselves, or new conquerors arrived from Greece. Another theory is that the Minoans rebelled against the Mycenaeans. Between 1400BC and 1100BC a joint Minoan-Mycenaean culture flourished, but Crete became a second-class power. By 1100BC Minoan culture had collapsed.

The Minotaur

According to a later Greek legend, an Athenian prince called Theseus went to Crete, where he fought and killed a terrible monster called the Minotaur. It was half man, half bull and was kept in a maze called the *Labyrinth*. *

Perhaps there was some truth in this story. The palace at Knossos might well have seemed like a maze because it had so many rooms and corridors. It could have been known as the *Labyrinth*, or house of the *labrys†*, because it was decorated with so many pictures of the double axe.

The Minotaur could also have been based on fact. One scholar has suggested that the king wore the mask of a bull's head during religious rituals. It is possible that the story may have become confused. People may have forgotten about the king and begun to believe in a monster.

Key dates

c.6000BC The first farmers arrive on Crete and the Greek mainland.

c.3000BC People in Greece discover how to make bronze. Start of the Bronze Age†.

c.2000BC The first palaces are built on Crete.

c.1900BC The Minoans start to use the Linear A† script.

c.1700BC The first palaces are destroyed by earthquake. New palaces are built.

c.1600BC The first Mycenaeans arrive on Crete.

c.1450BC Traditional date for the destruction of Thera. Recent evidence suggests that this date may have to be revised (see above).

c.1400BC Final destruction of the palace at Knossos.

c.1100BC End of Minoan culture.

* You can read the full story of Theseus and the Minotaur on page 82.

The Mycenaeans

From about 1600-1100BC, mainland Greece was dominated by a people we call the Mycenaeans, who lived in small kingdoms. Their name comes from the city of Mycenae, where remains of the culture were first discovered. Some experts believe that the Mycenaeans invaded Greece from central Europe between 2000-1900BC. Others think that they had already been in Greece for some time, and only gradually became the dominant people. Although they were never politically united, the Mycenaeans were linked by their culture. They all spoke an early form of the Greek language and they shared a common way of life and religious beliefs.

The Mycenaean cities, c.1200BC

Troy
Iolkos
Orchomenos • Gla
Thebes
Athens
Mycenae
Tiryns
Sparta
Pylos
Miletus

The royal graves

Some of the first and most important archaeological evidence about the Mycenaeans comes from the royal graves at Mycenae, which date from 1600BC. There were two main styles of grave: shaft graves and *tholos* tombs.

Shaft graves

The earliest tombs were shaft graves, like the one shown on this cutaway reconstruction. A shaft grave could be over 12 metres (40ft) deep and usually contained several bodies, perhaps from the same family.

Roof made from wooden beams and stone slabs.

A rectangular slab of stone called a *stele†* was used to mark the grave.

Chamber for the body and grave goods

When the grave was complete, the shaft was filled with earth.

Low stone walls

Pebble base

Tholos tombs

By about 1500BC, shaft graves had been replaced by the *tholos*, or beehive-shaped, tomb. This reconstruction shows one from Mycenae, which dates from c.1250BC. The Roman historian, Pausanias, thought these tombs were treasuries because of the rich grave goods they contained. This *tholos* is still called the Treasury of Atreus, after a legendary Mycenaean king.*

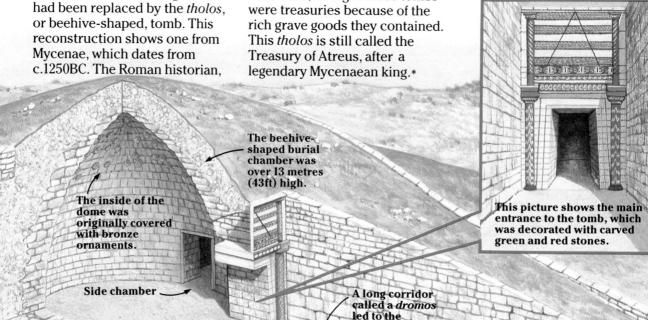

The inside of the dome was originally covered with bronze ornaments.

The beehive-shaped burial chamber was over 13 metres (43ft) high.

Side chamber

A long corridor called a *dromos* led to the entrance.

This picture shows the main entrance to the tomb, which was decorated with carved green and red stones.

Tomb treasure

Members of the royal families were buried with many precious objects. Shaft graves were difficult for tomb robbers to break into, and so have often survived with their goods intact. The objects shown here were all found in the graves at Mycenae.

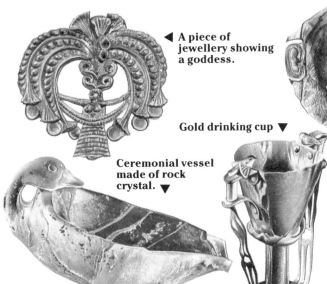

◄ A piece of jewellery showing a goddess.

Gold drinking cup ▼

Ceremonial vessel made of rock crystal. ▼

▲
The faces of some of the kings were covered with masks made of beaten gold. The masks were probably portraits of the kings.

▲
Sword and dagger blades were bronze, but the hilts were often made of gold.

Religion

There are no written records of the Mycenaeans' religious beliefs. Our only evidence comes from frescoes†, statues and shrines. From these it appears that the Mycenaeans had a very similar system of beliefs to the Minoans (see page 8).

◄ The Mycenaeans did not build temples, but there seem to have been rooms set aside for worship in houses and palaces. Shrines like the one shown on this gold ornament were erected in the countryside.

Mycenaean records mention several gods, such as ▶ Zeus, Poseidon and Dionysus, who were to be important in later Greek history. This fresco shows a figure holding ears of corn. She may be an early version of the goddess Demeter (see page 65).

Their elaborate tombs show that they believed in a life after death. They thought that goods from this world would be of use in the afterlife and would help wealthy people to preserve the privileges they had on Earth.

This terracotta† figurine represents a ▶ Mycenaean goddess. As in Crete, goddesses seem to have been the most powerful deities. A young male god is sometimes shown, but he seems to have been a less important figure.

Clothes

Statuettes and frescoes give us an idea of what fashions and hairstyles were like in Mycenaean days. They seem to have closely resembled the fashions on Crete. This fresco shows a court lady from Mycenae.

▼

▲
Young men, like the ones shown out hunting on this dagger blade, seem to have been clean shaven. Many of the gold masks from shaft graves show bearded men, but this may have been an older man's style.

Key dates

c.2000BC First evidence of the Mycenaeans in Greece.

c.1650-1550BC Grave circle A (see page 12) is in use at Mycenae.

c.1600BC The height of Mycenaean power, economy and culture.

c.1450BC The Mycenaeans occupy the palace of Knossos on Crete and become the rulers of the island (see page 9).

c.1250BC Defensive walls are built around many of the Mycenaean cities. Traditional date of the fall of Troy (see page 14).

c.1200BC Start of the period of Mycenaean decline. Their cities are gradually abandoned.

c.1100BC Start of the Dark Ages.

Mycenaean cities

The Mycenaeans lived in small kingdoms, each with its own city. Their cities were usually built on areas of high ground and were surrounded by walls to make them easy to defend. This type of fortified city is called an *acropolis*†, which means "high city" in Greek.

An *acropolis* contained a royal palace along with houses for courtiers, soldiers and craftsmen. The palace was not just a royal residence. It was also a military headquarters, the administrative centre from which the government was run, and a workplace for many skilled craftsmen.

The acropolis at Mycenae

The earliest Mycenaean cities were often destroyed when new ones were built on the same sites. The buildings shown in this view of the ruins at Mycenae were built at the end of the Mycenaean period.

The Lion Gate

The main gateway was decorated with sculptures of two lions. These may have been the symbols of the Mycenaean royal family. In about 1250BC enormous stone walls were built to enclose the *acropolis*. In some parts they were seven metres (23ft) thick.

City walls

The lion gate

Grave circle A

Houses

Grave circle A

A burial ground for members of the Mycenaean royal family, now known as grave circle A, was situated inside the city walls. It consisted of a number of shaft graves† (see page 10) enclosed by a low stone wall.

Writing

Clay tablets covered with writing have been found in some Mycenaean cities. The Mycenaeans learned the art of writing from the Minoans. They combined some signs from Linear A† (see page 5) with new signs to produce a script to suit their language. This is known as Linear B. Although experts are now able to read Linear B, the results have been disappointing as the tablets only give lists of goods and inhabitants in the palaces.

Mycenaean scribes at work

An example of Linear B script

Trade

The Mycenaeans were trading as early as the 16th century BC. At first, they had to compete with the Minoans, but they found more trading opportunities as Cretan power declined.

The Mycenaeans traded extensively in the eastern Mediterranean and kept trading posts in important cities along the coasts of Asia Minor and Lebanon. They also purchased items from more distant lands, such as Africa or Scandinavia, through other traders.

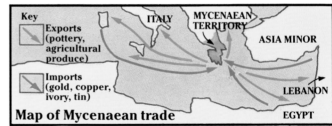

Key

Exports (pottery, agricultural produce)

Imports (gold, copper, ivory, tin)

ITALY
MYCENAEAN TERRITORY
ASIA MINOR
LEBANON
EGYPT

Map of Mycenaean trade

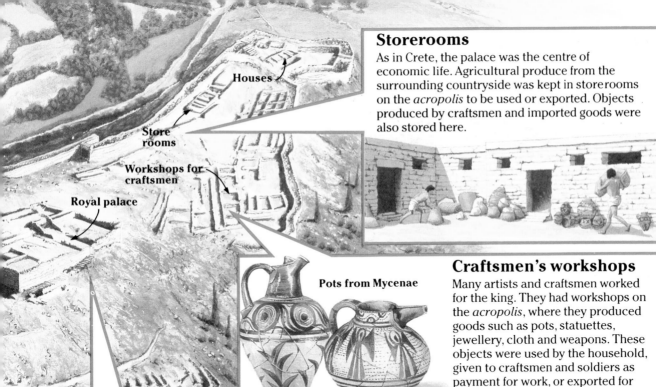

Houses

Store rooms

Workshops for craftsmen

Royal palace

Storerooms

As in Crete, the palace was the centre of economic life. Agricultural produce from the surrounding countryside was kept in storerooms on the *acropolis* to be used or exported. Objects produced by craftsmen and imported goods were also stored here.

Craftsmen's workshops

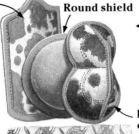

Pots from Mycenae

Many artists and craftsmen worked for the king. They had workshops on the *acropolis*, where they produced goods such as pots, statuettes, jewellery, cloth and weapons. These objects were used by the household, given to craftsmen and soldiers as payment for work, or exported for profit.

The royal palace

A Mycenaean palace consisted of a number of buildings, often more than one storey high, grouped around a central courtyard. It was brightly painted, both inside and out. In each palace there was a large hall called a *megaron*, where the king held court and conducted state business. Little remains of the *megaron* at Mycenae. This reconstruction is based on the remains from other palaces, which would have been similar.

The room contained four pillars and a hearth.

The walls were covered with frescoes†.

Warriors

The Mycenaeans seem to have been a very warlike people. We know from the weapons and armour found in graves that their kings and nobles were warriors. A ruler was expected to look after his soldiers, supplying them with food, housing, land and slaves. This was organized through the palace, where many warriors seem to have lived.

◀ Mycenaean soldiers used body armour, helmets and shields. This bronze armour was found in a grave. It must have belonged to a nobleman, as it would have been very expensive. Various types of helmet are shown on vases and frescoes. Most helmets had cheek flaps and were fastened under the chin. The one shown here was made of leather, covered with the tusks of wild boars.

Tower shield

Round shield

◀ The Mycenaeans used three styles of shield: the rectangular tower shape, the figure of eight shape and the round shape. They were made of oxhide stretched over a wooden frame.

Figure of eight shield

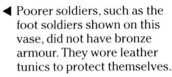

◀ Poorer soldiers, such as the foot soldiers shown on this vase, did not have bronze armour. They wore leather tunics to protect themselves.

We know very little about how a ▶ Mycenaean army was organized. It seems that rulers and nobles fought from chariots drawn by two horses. Each chariot contained a driver and a warrior.

The Trojan War

The story of the Trojan War is told in the works of the Greek poet, Homer†. He describes how a city called Troy was destroyed by the Mycenaean Greeks after a ten year siege. For many years historians thought that the Trojan War was just a story. However, at the end of the 19th century AD the remains of Troy were discovered in modern Turkey, and many experts now think that there is some truth in Homer's tale. Although we still cannot prove that Homer's Trojan War happened, some experts now believe that a war on which his story was based may have taken place around 1250BC.

This reconstruction shows the city of Troy under siege from the Greeks.

The legend of the Trojan War

The cause of the war between Greece and Troy was Helen of Sparta. She was so beautiful that all the Greek kings wanted to marry her. Helen eventually married Menelaus, brother of King Agamemnon of Mycenae. Her father made all her suitors swear an oath to support Menelaus and to help if anyone tried to kidnap Helen.

Unfortunately, Aphrodite, the goddess of love and beauty, promised Helen to Paris, a prince of Troy. She made Helen fall in love with him, and the pair eloped to live in Troy. Agamemnon was angered by his brother's humiliation. He reminded the other Greek kings of their oath, and organized a great military expedition to Troy to get Helen back.

Troy was a heavily fortified city and could not be easily defeated. For ten years the Greeks laid siege to the city and the battle raged. Heroes on both sides displayed great bravery. Then Odysseus, the King of Ithaca, thought of a trick to help them seize Troy.

They built a huge wooden horse, left it outside the city and then sailed away. When they had gone, the Trojans brought the horse into the city,

thinking that it would bring them luck.

That night Greek soldiers, who were concealed inside the hollow horse, crept out and opened the city gates. The Greek army, which had sneaked back under cover of darkness, charged in and destroyed the city. They killed the men and made the women and children slaves. Only one Trojan prince, Aeneas, escaped alive with his family. He fled to Italy, where his descendants are said to have founded the city of Rome.

The search for Troy

At the end of the 19th century AD, a German called Heinrich Schliemann set out to discover the city of Troy. He had complete faith in the accuracy of Homer's account, and he used the descriptions in Homer's poem, the *Iliad*, to locate the site of the city.

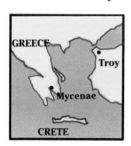

A picture of the wooden horse, taken from a Greek vase.

In AD 1870 Schliemann started to dig at a site called Hisarlik, in modern Turkey. He uncovered the ruins of a city, which he believed to be Troy. Several archaeological expeditions have since excavated the site. We now know that the city was built c.3600BC, but it was rebuilt at least eight times. Experts disagree about which of the layers is the city described in the *Iliad*.

Several of the cities uncovered at Hisarlik were destroyed violently, but we do not know whether this was by earthquake or war. People from the Greek mainland may well have raided Troy and destroyed the city, but there is not yet any archaeological evidence to prove that the Trojan War took place in the way Homer described.

The end of the age

By about 1200BC the Mycenaean world was breaking up. Egyptian records show that in the second half of the 13th century BC there was a long run of poor harvests, food shortages and then famine. In Mycenaean Greece, bad harvests would also have affected trade, as agricultural produce was exported and used to pay craftsmen. Without it, the whole economic system and way of life was threatened (see diagram).

The economic system

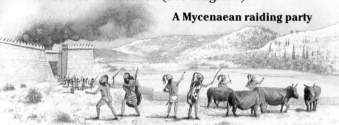

A Mycenaean raiding party

In times of shortage, the Mycenaeans traditionally attacked their neighbours to steal their cattle and crops. Enormous stone walls were built around many cities at this time and may well have been intended as protection against marauding neighbours. Some groups of Mycenaeans may also have gone on raids overseas. This may have been the real cause of the war against Troy.

The Sea Peoples

The famine may have driven some Mycenaeans to emigrate. Egyptian texts show that in about 1190BC a group of emigrants were reported in the eastern Mediterranean. Some were travelling overland with their women and children, while others were at sea in a large battle fleet. The Egyptians called them the Sea Peoples. Some of the Sea Peoples seem to have been Mycenaean refugees.

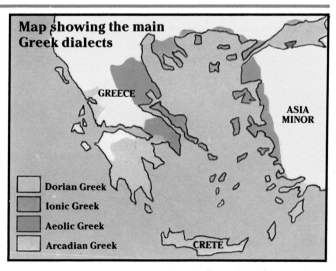

A reconstruction of a battle between the Egyptians and the Sea Peoples, based on an Egyptian relief†.

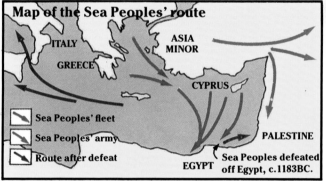

Map of the Sea Peoples' route

ITALY
GREECE
ASIA MINOR
CYPRUS
PALESTINE
EGYPT

Sea Peoples' fleet

Sea Peoples' army

Route after defeat

Sea Peoples defeated off Egypt, c.1183BC.

The Sea Peoples' fleet seized Cyprus, while their army destroyed several cities and defeated a people called the Hittites in Asia Minor. The fleet and army were eventually defeated by the Egyptian Pharaoh, Ramesses III. After this the Sea Peoples dispersed around the Mediterranean. Some may have been the ancestors of the Etruscans in Italy and of the Philistines in Palestine.

The Dorians

One by one, the Mycenaean cities were abandoned. Some may have been ruined by earthquakes, while others were destroyed by enemies. As the Mycenaean world disintegrated, Greece entered the Dark Ages (see page 16) and a people called the Dorians came to prominence.

It was once thought that the Dorians invaded from outside Greece. However, many experts now think that they had been in Greece for some time, but took advantage of the troubled times to exert their influence. In the places where they settled, the Dorian dialect of Greek was later spoken. Different dialects developed in other areas (see map).

Map showing the main Greek dialects

GREECE
ASIA MINOR
CRETE

Dorian Greek

Ionic Greek

Aeolic Greek

Arcadian Greek

The Dark Ages: c.1100-800BC

This period is known as the Dark Ages because we know very little of what was happening in Greece. The art of writing was lost after the end of the Mycenaean civilization, so there are no written records. There is also little mention of the Greeks in foreign records, as they had very few contacts with other countries. By the beginning of the Dark Ages the population had decreased dramatically. There was a general decline in the standard of pottery, jewellery and architecture. Skills such as fresco† painting and cutting gems were forgotten.

Many farming communities were destroyed during the disturbances at the end of the Mycenaean period.

Architecture

In the Dark Ages the main building materials were mud brick (mud mixed with straw and left in the sun to dry) and wood. These materials do not last as well as stone, so very few buildings have survived. Most people probably lived in small huts like the one shown in the reconstruction below.

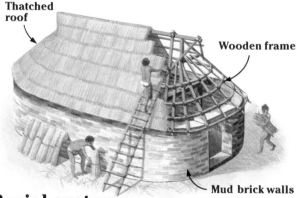

Thatched roof

Wooden frame

Mud brick walls

Clothes

Many dress pins from the Dark Ages have been discovered. They suggest that fashions were very different from the tightly laced and tied Mycenaean clothes. People started to wear simple, loose tunics, made from rectangular pieces of cloth, fastened at the shoulders with pins. This style is known as the Doric *chiton*.

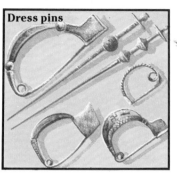

Dress pins

Woman wearing a Doric *chiton*.

Burial customs

Archaeological evidence from a cemetery in Athens has shown that cremation was introduced in the Dark Ages. The body was burned and the ashes were put in a clay jar in the grave. By about 800BC burial was once more in favour.

The Dark Age Greeks continued the Mycenaean custom of burying objects with the dead. However, people could not usually afford to bury luxury goods and most graves contained just a pottery jug or cup.

A vase painting of a funeral. It shows the dead person on a bed, surrounded by mourners who are tearing their hair in grief.

Euboea

On the island of Euboea, excavations have revealed a flourishing Dark Age culture. It was rich enough for people to put gold ornaments in their graves. As early as 900BC, the Euboeans were re-establishing trading contacts with foreign countries. However, wars between the two main cities on Euboea ended this period of progress.

These objects were all discovered in tombs on Euboea.

Terracotta† figure of a centaur

Pot decorated with human figures

Gold rings and earrings

Euboea

Athens

The Archaic Period: c.800-500BC

The Archaic Period was a time of progress and expansion. The population grew and there was a rise in the general standard of living. The standard of art improved and the Greeks had more contact with the outside world. The first Olympic Games were held in this period (see page 58).

The rediscovery of writing

About 800BC the Greeks started to use writing again. They had trading links with a people called the Phoenicians, who used an alphabet which contained only consonants. The Greeks adapted this by introducing extra signs for vowels. This system of writing was very successful, as it was much easier to learn than previous scripts.
It is the predecessor of the alphabet we use today.

Greek letter, name of letter and English sound

α alpha a	β beta b	γ gamma g	δ delta d	ε epsilon e	ζ zeta z	η eta e	θ theta th
ι iota i	κ kappa k	λ lambda l	μ mu m	ν nu n	ξ xi x/ks	ο omicron o	π pi p
ρ rho r	σ, ς sigma s	τ tau t	υ upsilon u	φ phi f/ph	χ chi ch	ψ psi ps	ω omega o

Bards

A bard reciting his poem.

Although no written records were kept during the Dark Ages, the people had a very strong oral tradition. Professional poets, known as bards, travelled widely, passing on the stories of the gods and the Mycenaean heroes.

The most famous bard is Homer†, whose poems are the earliest surviving example of Greek literature. We know very little about Homer's life. He may have come from the island of Chios, and tradition maintains that he was blind. Some time between 850-750BC, Homer retold the traditional stories about the Trojan War (see page 14). He composed two epic poems: the *Iliad* (the story of part of the siege of Troy) and the *Odyssey* (the account of the hero Odysseus' journey home to Ithaca). *

Roman bust of Homer, based on a Greek original.

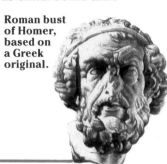

Emigration

As the population started to grow, some areas of Greece became overcrowded and sometimes there were famines. Political struggles between the various Greek states also created exiles and refugees who were forced to flee abroad. From about 1000BC onwards, groups of people left Greece seeking land or employment overseas. The first emigrants travelled to the coastal area of Asia Minor, which was called Ionia. Later groups settled all round the Mediterranean, from France to the Black Sea. They settled in places with natural harbours and good farming land, where they faced little opposition from the local inhabitants. Once a colony was established, it rapidly became independent from the mother city.

Map of the Greek colonies

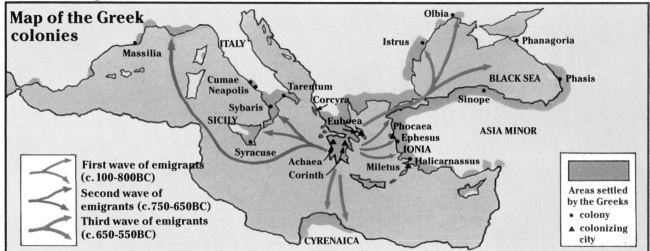

Olbia
Istrus
Phanagoria
Massilia
ITALY
BLACK SEA
Phasis
Cumae
Neapolis
Tarentum
Corcyra
Sinope
Sybaris
SICILY
Euboea
Phocaea
Ephesus
ASIA MINOR
Syracuse
IONIA
Achaea
Halicarnassus
Corinth
Miletus
CYRENAICA

First wave of emigrants (c. 100-800BC)
Second wave of emigrants (c. 750-650BC)
Third wave of emigrants (c. 650-550BC)

Areas settled by the Greeks
• colony
▲ colonizing city

The Greeks and their neighbours

During the Dark Ages, the Greeks had few contacts with the outside world. However, from the Archaic Period onwards, when they started to set up colonies and to trade, they came into contact with many peoples around the Mediterranean. Some of them are described below.

The Assyrians

During the Dark Ages a people called the Assyrians conquered a vast area of the Middle East. They came from the area that is now Iraq and their most important cities were Ashur (the capital) and Nineveh.

This stone carving shows the Assyrian king Ashurbanipal out hunting.

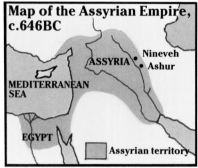

Map of the Assyrian Empire, c.646BC

ASSYRIA
Nineveh
Ashur
MEDITERRANEAN SEA
EGYPT
Assyrian territory

The Assyrians were a warlike people, famed for their cruelty. Archaeologists have discovered lists of Assyrian kings going back to 2500BC. However, it was not until around 1814BC that they started to expand their territory. Their empire reached its height in about 646BC under King Ashurbanipal.

The Egyptians

There were many trading links between Egypt and the Greeks. The Greeks purchased papyrus for scrolls, fine linen, perfumes and wine from the Egyptians. They also kept trading posts in the Egyptian cities of Naucratis and Daphnae.

The pyramids at Giza were built in the 26th century BC and were tombs for Egyptian kings.

By the time of the Greek Dark Ages, the Egyptian civilization had been in existence for over 2000 years. In c.1190BC Pharaoh Ramesses III defeated the Sea Peoples (see page 15). However, under his successors Egyptian power started to decline. The country was later conquered by Alexander the Great† (see pages 74-75) and in 30BC it became part of the Roman Empire.

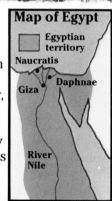

Map of Egypt

Egyptian territory
Naucratis
Daphnae
Giza
River Nile

The Etruscans

In about 750BC, the Greeks started to set up colonies in southern Italy. There they came into conflict with a people called the Etruscans, who were expanding their territory southward from north-western Italy. Some scholars believe that the Etruscans were native inhabitants of Italy. Others think that they were Sea Peoples who had to find a new home after they were defeated by the Egyptians. They may even have come from Asia Minor.

The Etruscans were expert sailors, who traded extensively around the Mediterranean. They were also skilled metalworkers. Their engineers knew how to build sewage systems for their towns and drain marshy areas.

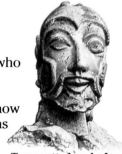

Terracotta head of an Etruscan warrior

Etruscan statue from a temple built in the 3rd century BC.

Bronze statue of a mythical beast called a *chimera*.

Map of Etruscan territory

Alalia
Rome
Capua
Cumae

Original Etruscan territory
Etruscan expansion
Greek colonies

Key dates

c.900BC Etruscan cities are founded in north-west Italy.

c.600BC Etruscans found the city of Capua and clash with Greek colonists at Cumae.

c.540BC Etruscans defeat the Greeks in a naval battle at Alaliah and gain control of Corsica and the north-west Mediterranean.

474BC Greeks defeat the Etruscans in a naval battle off Cumae. Etruscans lose control of the north-west Mediterranean.

358-262BC Romans conquer the Etruscan cities.

The Phoenicians

During the Greek Dark Ages, the most successful traders in the Mediterranean were a people called the Phoenicians. They lived on the coast in what is now the Lebanon. The Greeks called them *Phoinikes*, or purple men, after a purple dye which they produced. Their most important exports were purple cloth, timber, glass and goods made of metal and wood, including fine furniture inlaid with ivory.

The Phoenicians lived in independent city states, each of which had its own king. Their most

A Phoenician trading ship leaving port.

important cities were Byblos, Sidon and Tyre. They were daring sailors and explorers and established colonies round the south and west shores of the Mediterranean (see map).

In about 1000BC the Phoenicians invented a form of writing. Their alphabet was later adopted by the Greeks (see page 17).

Phoenician pots made from coloured glass.

Map of the Phoenician colonies

ITALY

GREECE

PHOENICIA
Sidon
Byblos

Carthage

Tyre

EGYPT

Areas colonized by the Phoenicians

Key dates

c.1200-1000BC Phoenicians rise to power.

c.814BC Princess Elissa of Tyre founds the colony of Carthage on the North African coast.

c.600BC Phoenician sailors circumnavigate Africa.

539BC Phoenicia is conquered by the Persians (see page 41).

332BC Phoenicia is conquered by Alexander the Great (see pages 74-75)

The Lydians

Lydian coin

Lydia was a small but wealthy state in Asia Minor. Its capital was Sardis. The Lydians were close neighbours of the Ionian Greek colonies, with whom they traded.

Key dates

c.680-652BC Reign of King Gyges. He starts a policy of attacking the Ionian Greek colonies, while trying to maintain friendly relations with mainland Greece.

7th century BC The Lydians are the first people to use coins.

560-546BC Reign of King Croesus. In alliance with a people called the Medes, he conquers the Ionian colonies.

546BC Croesus is defeated by the Persians. The Persians seize the Ionian colonies (see page 40).

Lydian and Scythian territory

Greek colonies

Scythian territory

Lydian territory

BLACK SEA

ASIA MINOR

GREECE

The Scythians

The Scythians were a tribe of nomadic horsemen from Central Asia who kept herds of horses, cattle and sheep. In about 1000BC, they moved into the area around the Black Sea.

The Scythians were a barbaric and warlike people. Greek colonists who settled around the Black Sea often had to defend their territory against them. However, a lot of trade was done between the two peoples. The Greeks bought wheat, salt, hides and slaves from the Scythians,

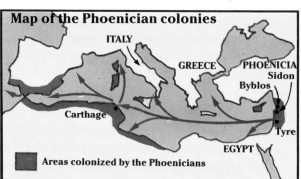

A Scythian chief, noblewoman and horse in their ceremonial costumes

and in return supplied them with jewellery, metalwork, oils and wines. The Scythians were a very wealthy people. Their graves were filled with rich goods, along with human and horse sacrifices.

Greek craftsmen made many pieces of gold jewellery for the Scythians.

Earring

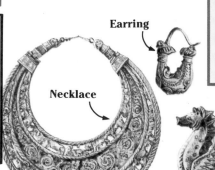

Necklace

Ornament for clothes

Key dates

674BC The Scythians make an alliance with the Assyrians.

c.650BC The Scythians and Assyrians plunder various areas of the Middle East.

c.630BC The Scythians defeat a people called the Cimmerians from central Asia.

514BC The Scythians repel the Persians.

Social structure and government

In the Archaic Period, Greece was made up of many independent states. The Greeks called each of these a *polis*, or city state. A *polis* consisted of the city and its surrounding countryside. The largest *polis* was Athens, which had about 2,500 square kilometres (1,000 squares miles) of territory. However, most states were much smaller, many with less than 250 square kilometres (100 square miles).

The Greeks liked to keep each city state small. Even the largest city states had no more than a few thousand citizens (see below). This reconstruction shows what a typical *polis* would have looked like in the Archaic Period.

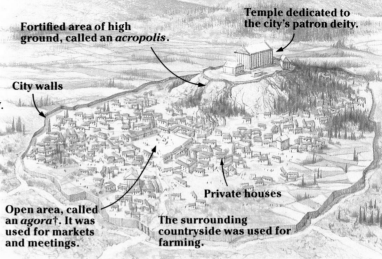

Fortified area of high ground, called an *acropolis*.

Temple dedicated to the city's patron deity.

City walls

Private houses

Open area, called an *agora*†. It was used for markets and meetings.

The surrounding countryside was used for farming.

Social structure

In Greek society there were always two main groups of people: free people and slaves. Slaves were workers who were owned by free people. They were used as servants and labourers and had no legal rights. Some slaves were prisoners of war from other Greek states. Others were foreigners purchased from slave traders. Many slaves worked closely with their owners and lived as members of the family. A few slaves were skilled craftsmen and were paid for their work.

Female slaves doing basic housework.

Male slaves at work on a farm.

In Athens, as society developed, free men (but not women) became divided into two groups: citizens and *metics*. A citizen was a free man, born to Athenian parents. Citizens were the most powerful and privileged group. They were the only people who could take part in the government of the *polis*. They had to serve in the army, and were also expected to be government officials and to volunteer for jury service (see pages 60-61).

A *metic* was a man born outside Athens who had come to live there, usually to trade or to practise a craft. Many of them were very prosperous. *Metics* had to pay tax and to serve in the army if required, but they could never become citizens. They had no say in the government, could not own houses or land and could not speak in a law court.

Metics often worked as jewellers, potters or smiths.

A man born into one of these social groups could rarely move into another one. This rigid social system was enforced by a law passed in Athens in 451BC, which defined who could be a citizen. The only people who could sometimes improve their social status were slaves.

Occasionally, a master would pay to set a skilled slave up in business. He would receive a share of the profits in return. Some of these wage-earning slaves were able to save up and buy their freedom. However, freed slaves could never become citizens or *metics*.

A slave receiving his freedom.

All these social divisions applied only to men. Women took their social and legal status from their husband or male relations. They were not permitted to take part in public life.

Changing forms of government

Rule by the aristocrats: c.800-650BC

By the Archaic Period, most Greek states were governed by groups of rich landowners, called aristocrats. The word comes from the Greek *aristoi*, meaning "best people". This system of government is known as an *oligarchy*, which means "rule by the few" in Greek. As trade increased, a middle class of merchants, craftsmen and bankers began to prosper. However, they could not take part in government, and soon began to demand a say in the decision making.

In the early days aristocrats were the only people who could afford to buy armour and horses. They became leaders in war and at home.

The age of tyrants: c.650-500BC

Resentment of aristocratic power often led to riots. To re-establish peace, people were sometimes prepared to allow one man to take absolute power. This sort of leader was called a tyrant, which meant "ruler". Tyrants first appeared in about 650BC. They often tried to curb the power of the aristocrats, as this helped to protect their own positions. Some tyrants stayed in power for many years, but most only ruled for a short time.

Many tyrants were deposed by men who envied their power and wanted to be tyrants themselves.

Government in Athens: c.750-621BC

During the Archaic Period, real power in Athens lay with the *areopagus*, or council, whose policies were carried out by three magistrates called *archons*†. All the *archons* and the members of the council were aristocrats.

Many people were dissatisfied with this system and with the city's laws. In about 630BC, an aristocrat called Cylon tried to make himself tyrant, but failed. Instead the Athenians looked for someone to reform their laws, and in 621BC they appointed a man called Draco†. He drew up a new set of laws which were very severe.

Draco's laws were so harsh that even minor crimes such as stealing food were punished by death. A harsh law is still referred to as "draconian".

Solon's reforms

People were unhappy with Draco's laws. In 594BC an aristocrat called Solon† was made *archon* and given power to introduce reforms. Many of Solon's measures were very popular. For example, he prevented merchants selling grain abroad, which meant there was more food for the Athenian poor. He cancelled many debts and stopped debtors being sold into slavery. Solon also reformed the system of government, so that men from the middle classes could hold administrative positions. Even poor citizens were given a say in the city's affairs through an Assembly (see page 60).

Solon arranged for debtors to be freed. Some were brought home from abroad.

The tyrant of Athens

Despite these reforms, few people were satisfied. Solon left Athens and disorder broke out again between the aristocratic families and the various social groups. About 546BC, an aristocrat called Peisistratus† seized power and became the tyrant of Athens. His rule was largely a success, and he appears to have been popular. Under his rule, Athens enjoyed a period of peace and prosperity.

Peisistratus tried to take power several times. Once he arrived in Athens with a woman dressed as Athene. He hoped to persuade people that the goddess had appointed him leader.

The introduction of democracy

When Peisistratus died in 527BC, his son Hippias became tyrant. He ruled until 510BC, when he was overthrown. Two years of civil war followed. An aristocrat called Cleisthenes†, from a family called the Alcmaeonids, eventually triumphed. In 508BC he introduced a new system of government called *democracy* (see pages 60-61).

Hippias was deposed by members of the Alcmaeonid family, helped by Spartan troops.

Sparta

In the 10th century BC, people called Dorians moved into Laconia, a province of southern Greece. They defeated the native inhabitants and founded the state of Sparta. Between c.740-720BC, the Spartans conquered the neighbouring state of Messenia. This made Sparta one of the largest Greek states and gave it enough fertile land to make it self-sufficient in food.

By the beginning of the Archaic Period, the Spartans were trading with other Greek states and importing luxury goods from abroad. Their craftsmen produced fine metalware and they also had skilled vase painters. In the intellectual field, the Spartans are said to have played a leading role in the invention of Greek music, and they had a famous poet called Alcman.

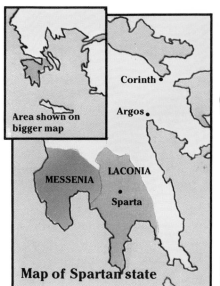

Corinth

Argos

Area shown on bigger map

MESSENIA   LACONIA

Sparta

Map of Spartan state

Bronze figure of a Spartan warrior, 5th century BC.

This scene is taken from the neck of a huge bronze pot known as the Vix krater (see page 48). It was made in Sparta in the 6th century BC and shows Spartan soldiers marching to war.

In 668BC the Spartans were defeated in a war against Argos. Then, in about 630BC, the Messenians started a revolt against the Spartans, which lasted for 17 years. These events convinced the Spartans that they must make drastic changes in order to keep the rebellious population under control and to defend themselves against any possible foreign invasion.

They set up a system dedicated to producing warriors. Every male Spartan had to become a full-time soldier and spent his life training and fighting. Spartans lived in very hard and uncomfortable conditions, without any luxuries. They distrusted any form of change and had as little contact with the outside world as possible.

By the Classical Period, Sparta had become the strongest military power in Greece, and its soldiers were famous for their bravery. However, this was achieved at the expense of its cultural development. There were now no philosophers or artists in Sparta.

This Spartan plate was made in c.560BC.

Social structure

Only men of Spartan birth were regarded as citizens†. They were an exclusive group who never admitted any outsiders, and there were probably never more than 9000 of them. All citizens served in the army and could vote in the assembly.

Men who were not full citizens were known as *perioikoi*, which meant "neighbours". Although they were under Spartan rule, they were free men who were allowed to trade and to serve in the army. They lived in separate small villages.

Descendants of Sparta's original inhabitants were known as *helots*. They farmed the land and had to give part of their crops to their Spartan masters. The *helots* outnumbered the Spartans heavily. The Spartans kept them oppressed, to prevent rebellions.

Life in Sparta

Physical fitness was very important to the Spartans, as only strong and healthy men could become soldiers. Each new baby had to be examined by state officials. If it showed signs of weakness it was left outside to die.

A boy was educated by the state until he was 20 (see pages 52-53). Then he had to join the army and be elected into one of the military clubs. He lived and ate in the club's barracks, where conditions were very harsh.

Each soldier was allocated land and *helots* to work it by the state. This left him free to pursue his military career. He supported his family and helped to supply his barracks from the produce of his land.

Spartan men did not usually marry until they were 30. Even then they spent most of their time at the barracks, and just visited their wives and families. Only old men were allowed to live in their own homes.

Spartan women had to keep fit so that they would give birth to strong babies. They trained and competed against each other in athletic events, wearing short tunics. Other Greeks were often shocked by this behaviour.

Foreigners were not allowed into Sparta. Only the *perioikoi*, who looked after trade, had any dealings with outsiders. The Spartans did not use coins and usually bartered for goods.

Government in Sparta

The Spartan system of government included a monarchy, a council of elders and a popular assembly. Their various functions are shown on this diagram. According to legend, a leader called Lycurgus set up the government institutions and laws. Experts now disagree about whether or not he was a real historical character.

Sparta had two royal families and two kings, who always ruled together. Their main responsibility was to lead the army in war. At home, their powers were strictly limited to religious duties.

More actual power lay with the five *ephors*, or overseers, who were elected annually by the Assembly (see below). They looked after the day-to-day running of the state.

The *gerousia*, or Council, was made up of the two kings and 28 councillors. Councillors were men over 60 who had been elected for life by the Assembly. The councillors decided which policies Sparta should adopt. They also created the laws and acted as judges.

The Council's proposals had to be passed by the *apella*, or Assembly, which consisted of all citizens aged over 30. The Assembly could not debate or amend a measure, it could only vote for or against it. Spartans voted by shouting "yes" or "no": the loudest group would win.

The Peloponnesian League

The Spartans realized that they did not have enough soldiers to fight an enemy abroad and suppress a *helot* uprising at the same time. In the 6th century BC, they therefore made a series of alliances with their neighbours in the Peloponnese (the southern part of mainland Greece). This is known as the Peloponnesian League. Sparta's allies remained independent, but they had to give Sparta military assistance when required.

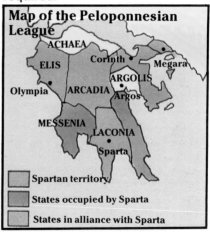

Map of the Peloponnesian League

ACHAEA
ELIS
Corinth
Megara
ARGOLIS
Olympia
ARCADIA
Argos
MESSENIA
LACONIA
Sparta

☐ Spartan territory
☐ States occupied by Sparta
☐ States in alliance with Sparta

Farming and food

Most people in Ancient Greece made their living from farming. Even the citizens of towns often had a farm in the country which provided their income. However, the landscape and climate of Greece made farming difficult. About three-quarters of the land area was mountainous and therefore of little use for agriculture. Land could be farmed on the coastal plain and in some inland areas, and in places the soil was very fertile. Only a few areas, such as Thessaly, had good pasture land. Very little rain fell between March and October, so crops were grown during the winter.

A Greek farm

This scene shows a typical Greek farm. They were usually quite small, and only produced enough food to support a single family. They were worked by the owner, his family and a few hired hands or slaves. If the owner lived mostly in the town, he paid a servant called a bailiff to run the farm.

Areas of high ground or poor soil, which were useless for other crops, could be used to grow olive trees.

Grapes were grown in vineyards on the lower hill slopes.

Farm buildings

Grain was grown on the fertile plains. It was the most important crop, as bread was the main element in the Greek diet.

Many farmers kept animals (see below). They grazed on the hillside and were looked after by one of the farm workers.

Farmers grew fruit and vegetables to feed their families.

Farm animals

Many horses were reared in Thessaly, where there was lots of pasture land. Elsewhere they were expensive to keep and were only used by the rich.

Oxen were used to draw the plough and mules were kept as beasts of burden.

In fertile areas cows were kept for their milk.

Fish were plentiful and many varieties were found in the seas around Greece.

Farmers often kept pigs and poultry for their meat.

Most milk came from sheep and goats. They were also eaten, and their hides were used for leather.

24

Grapes

Grapes were picked in September. Some were kept for eating, but most were made into wine. They were trodden underfoot in big vats. This first squeezing of the grapes made the best quality wine. The last drops of juice were extracted in a press. The juice was then left in jars to ferment.

Olives

An olive press

The picture on this vase shows the olive harvest.

Olives were either picked by hand or knocked out of the trees with sticks. Some olives were eaten, but most were crushed in a press to produce oil. Olive oil was an essential product. It was used for cooking, lighting and in many beauty products. In the state of Athens it was a criminal offence to uproot an olive tree.

The grain harvest

1. Grain was sown in October, so that it could grow during the wettest months of the year. One man steered a wooden plough, pulled by oxen. Another man walked behind him, sowing the seeds.

2. In April or May, the crops were harvested with curved knives called sickles. Afterwards the field was left fallow (unplanted) for a while so that the soil could regain its goodness.

3. The grain was threshed (separated from the stalks), by driving mules over it on a paved threshing floor. Some floors were positioned so that the wind would blow away the chaff (the outer cover of the grain).

4. The grain could also be separated from the chaff by throwing it into the air, so that the chaff would blow away. This is known as winnowing. The husks were then removed by pounding the grain in a pestle and mortar.

What people ate

Most people in Greece lived mainly on porridge and bread. This was usually barley bread, as wheat was more expensive than barley. Other common foods were cheese, fish, vegetables, eggs and fruit. Wild animals such as hares, deer and boars were hunted to supplement the food supply. A typical day's food is shown in the picture on the right.

Coriander and sesame were popular seasonings. Bees were kept in terracotta† hives to provide honey, which was the only form of sweetening.

Rich people had a more varied diet. They ate more fish and meat and could afford bread made from wheat.

Breakfast usually consisted of a lump of bread soaked in wine.

The main meal of the day was dinner. This was often barley porridge or bread with some vegetables.

Lunch might be bread with a piece of cheese or some olives and figs.

A Greek house

Very few Greek houses have survived, so we cannot be sure exactly what a typical house looked like. We do know that Greek houses were usually built around a central courtyard from which doors opened into the various ground floor rooms. Any windows on the outside walls of the house tended to be small and could be closed with shutters. This made the house very private and secure. Stairs led from the courtyard to an upper storey, where the bedrooms and servants' quarters were situated. Men and women lived separate lives and had separate rooms within the house.

This reconstruction is based on the remains of a house found in the city of Olynthos. Some walls have been cut away to show the layout of the rooms. Not all the activities shown in this picture would have happened at the same time.

The roof was made of pottery tiles.

The women's quarters were called the *gynaeceum*. Women spent most of their time in these rooms, organizing the household, spinning, weaving and entertaining their friends.

The exterior

The outside walls were built from mud bricks, sometimes reinforced with timber. These bricks were cheap and easy to use, but they were not very strong. Burglars sometimes broke into houses by tunnelling through the walls. Doors and shutters were made of wood with bronze hinges. Wood was a valuable material, as it was very scarce.

A statue of the god Hermes, called a *herm*, often stood by the main entrance to the house to ward off evil. Wealthy people often employed a doorman to receive visitors.

Herm

The men ate and entertained their friends in a room called the *andron*. They reclined on couches and were served by slaves.

Mosaic floors were used in some rooms from the 5th century BC. They were made from coloured pebbles.

Heating was provided by burning charcoal in portable metal braziers.

Furniture

Furniture was usually made of wood. Rich people had more highly decorated furniture, which was often finely carved with inlays of ivory, gold and silver. Some items were made of bronze.

Chairs

A *thronos* was a seat of honour used by the master of the house. It was a large chair with arms.

The ladies used chairs with backs. This style was called a *klismos*.

Most people sat on stools. The legs could be fixed or folding.

Tables

Tables could be round, oval or rectangular and were usually low, so that they could be pushed under couches when not in use. They either had three legs or a single central support.

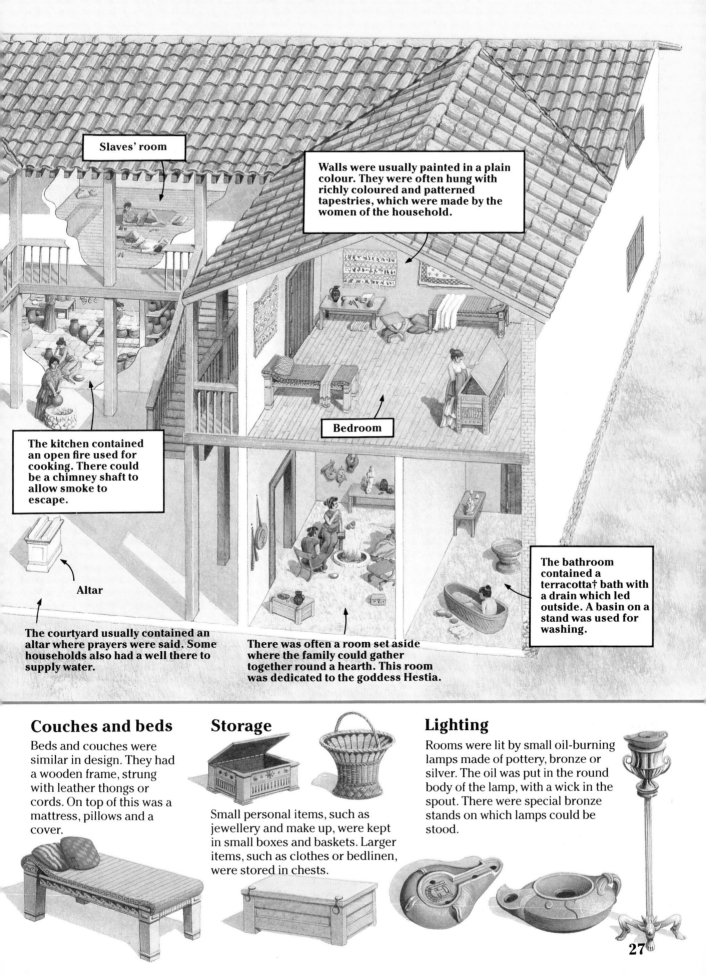

Slaves' room

Walls were usually painted in a plain colour. They were often hung with richly coloured and patterned tapestries, which were made by the women of the household.

The kitchen contained an open fire used for cooking. There could be a chimney shaft to allow smoke to escape.

Bedroom

Altar

The courtyard usually contained an altar where prayers were said. Some households also had a well there to supply water.

There was often a room set aside where the family could gather together round a hearth. This room was dedicated to the goddess Hestia.

The bathroom contained a terracotta† bath with a drain which led outside. A basin on a stand was used for washing.

Couches and beds

Beds and couches were similar in design. They had a wooden frame, strung with leather thongs or cords. On top of this was a mattress, pillows and a cover.

Storage

Small personal items, such as jewellery and make up, were kept in small boxes and baskets. Larger items, such as clothes or bedlinen, were stored in chests.

Lighting

Rooms were lit by small oil-burning lamps made of pottery, bronze or silver. The oil was put in the round body of the lamp, with a wick in the spout. There were special bronze stands on which lamps could be stood.

27

Clothes and jewellery

Greek clothes were very simple. Both men and women wore pieces of material draped around their bodies to form either a tunic or a cloak.

Clothes were usually made of wool or linen. However, in the 5th century BC the Greeks also started to use cotton, which came from India. By the 4th century BC silk was being produced on the island of Kos. Other luxury cloths were imported from Egypt, Persia and Phoenicia. Only the rich could afford any of these exotic materials. The poor wore clothes of poorer quality materials, such as undyed or unbleached wool and linen.

Women's clothes

The basic female dress was called a *chiton*. It was made from a single rectangular piece of cloth.

There were two main styles of *chiton*, the Doric and the Ionic.

The *chiton* was fastened with buttons or brooches.

A girdle could be tied around the waist.

The Doric *chiton* originated on mainland Greece. The top quarter of the material was folded over and it was then wrapped around the body, leaving one side open.

The *chiton* was fastened on the shoulders with long pins or brooches.

A girdle was often tied around the waist.

The Ionic style of *chiton* was said to have been invented in the Greek colonies in Ionia. It was fastened at intervals across the shoulders.

A *himation* could be a light, gauzy scarf.

This travelling cloak was also a *himation*.

A woman's other basic item of clothing was a rectangular-shaped wrap called a *himation*. It varied considerably in size and thickness.

Changing fashions

Paintings on vases show that in the Archaic Period highly patterned, brightly coloured fabrics were fashionable and women's dresses tended to fit closely to the body.

In later years there was a reaction against too much display. Dresses were made of material of one colour, but sometimes had a band of colour or a small pattern at the edge. The garments fitted more loosely.

In the 4th century BC this trend was reversed. Patterned materials, including ones with gold ornaments sewn on to them, were in favour again. The materials were fine and clung more revealingly to the figure.

Men's clothes

Young men wore thigh-length tunics.

Old men and the rich usually wore ankle-length tunics.

Slave wearing a loincloth.

Greek men wore a simple kilt or a tunic sewn up at the side and fastened on one or both shoulders. Craftsmen and slaves often wore a loincloth.

Men also wore a *himation*. It was ▶ usually rectangular in shape but varied considerably in size and texture. Sometimes it was worn over a tunic.

The *himation* was wrapped around the body with the end thrown over one shoulder.

The *chlamys* was fastened with a pin or brooch.

◀ There was also a shorter cloak called a *chlamys*, which was usually worn by younger men, particularly for hunting or riding, or by soldiers.

Footwear

Leather sandal. The straps could be tied in many different styles.

Leather boots were often lined with felt or fur for warmth.

Leather shoe

Many people went barefoot most of the time, especially indoors. The most common footwear was leather sandals, although shoes were sometimes worn. Horsemen and travellers wore calf-length boots.

Hats

Both men and women wore hats with brims when they were outdoors to protect themselves from the sun.

Jewellery

Many pieces of Greek jewellery have survived in tombs, as it was the custom to bury a dead person's jewellery with them. Paintings, sculptures and lists from temples give us other details. Rich people had jewellery made of gold, silver, electrum† and ivory. Less wealthy people had jewellery made of bronze, lead, iron, bone and glass.

Greek jewellers worked gold into many different shapes and textures and sometimes added touches of enamel for colour. It was not until the Hellenistic Period that coloured stones were used to decorate jewellery.

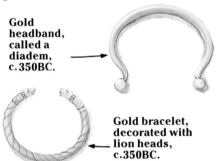

Gold headband, called a diadem, c.350BC.

Gold bracelet, decorated with lion heads, c.350BC.

Gold earrings, c.350BC.

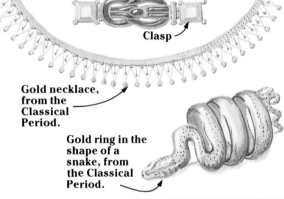

Clasp

Gold necklace, from the Classical Period.

Gold ring in the shape of a snake, from the Classical Period.

Hairstyles

In the Archaic Period, Greek men wore their hair long with a head band and they had full beards.

Hair styles became shorter during the Classical Period. Beards were also worn shorter.

In the Hellenistic Period it became fashionable for men to be clean-shaven.

Women always wore their hair long. In the Archaic Period it was held in place by a head band.

In the Classical Period hair was usually worn up, held in place by ribbons, diadems, nets or scarves.

In the Hellenistic Period, waves and curls were fashionable, although the hair was still usually worn up.

Pottery

Greek pottery was intended for everyday use. But as well as being functional, it was often beautifully decorated with paintings. The pictures on many pots show scenes from everyday life which have given us vital information about how the Greeks lived.

Styles of decoration

The Geometric Period: c.1000-700BC

During the Dark Ages the marine and plant decorations of the Bronze Age were abandoned in favour of geometric patterns. Early designs consisted of simple shapes such as zigzags and triangles. ▼

In the 9th and 8th centuries BC bands of decoration featuring animals and humans were added. The figures were shown as silhouettes against a light background and the scenes often depicted funerals. ▼

▲ In about 900BC very elaborate geometric patterns like this became common.

The Orientalizing and Archaic Periods: c.720-550BC

◄ As the Greeks started to have more contact with foreigners, oriental motifs such as lotuses, palms, lions and monsters became common on pottery.

In the Archaic Period, scenes from ► Greek mythology and from everyday life started to appear on pots. The figures were more detailed and realistic than those of the Geometric Period.

Athenian pottery: c.550-300BC

Athenian pottery dominated the market for over 200 years. The pictures on Athenian pots showed episodes from the lives of gods and heroes, as well as scenes from daily life.

At first, the ► Athenians made pottery known as black figure ware, which consisted of red pots decorated with black figures. This style was fashionable from about 550-480BC.

The Athenians also produced white pots with painted decorations. ►

▲ In about 530BC the Athenians developed red figure ware: black pots decorated with red figures. This style became very popular and eventually replaced the black figure style.

The Hellenistic Period: c.300BC onwards

In the Hellenistic Period, black and red figure ware were virtually abandoned in favour of plain coloured pots. These often had raised patterns on ◄ the pot.

Identifying shapes

Pots were made in many different shapes and sizes according to their use. Some of the most common styles of pot are shown here.

An *amphora* was a two-handled ▲ storage jar with a wide body and narrower neck. *Amphorae* were used to store wine, oil and many other commodities, and varied greatly in size and shape.

A *krater* was a large vase in which wine was mixed with water before it was served. Two different styles of *krater* are shown here. ▼

Volute krater

Calyx krater

The mixture of ▲ water and wine was transferred from the *krater* into a jug called an *oinochoe*, ready to be poured into wine cups.

How pots were made

Greek potters were skilled craftsmen who made a variety of things, including large storage jars, fine black and red figure ware, cooking pots, lamps and perhaps even roof tiles. The more decorative pots were usually made by two people (the potter and the artist who painted them), although sometimes one man did both jobs. Pots were often signed on the bottom by both the potter and the artist.

In Athens the potters had their own quarter, which was known as the *Kerameikos*. Potters' workshops were usually small and employed only five or six men. This reconstruction shows the inside of a typical workshop.

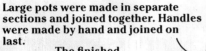

Large pots were made in separate sections and joined together. Handles were made by hand and joined on last.

The finished pot was decorated by a painter.

Pots were fired (baked) in a kiln like this one, which has been cut away to show how it worked.

Air vent

There was usually a hole in the loading door, so that the potter could see what was happening inside the kiln.

The finished pot, was turned upside down and smoothed to produce a fine surface.

Some Greek pots were moulded by hand, but most were made on a wheel. An apprentice often turned the wheel for the potter.

Wood or charcoal was burned here to heat the kiln.

Making black and red figure ware

This type of pottery was made from a clay that turned red when fired. The areas of the pot that were to be black were painted with black slip, a paint, made from clay, water and wood ash.

On black figure ware, details could be carved into the black surface so that they would show through in red. Touches of white and dark red paint were used to provide extra details.

At a certain point in the firing, all the vents and openings in the kiln were shut. This cut off the oxygen supply and caused a chemical reaction which turned the whole pot black.

The temperature was then allowed to drop and the vents were re-opened. The areas painted with the black slip stayed black, but the rest of the pot turned a clear red colour.

Skyphos

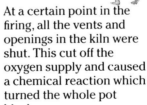

Water was fetched from the fountain in a jar called a *hydria*. It had three handles: two were used to lift it and the third to pour. ▼

Kylix

Kantharos

▲
A *kantharos*, a *kylix* and a *skyphos* were all drinking cups. They had big handles so that people lying on couches could hold them easily.

Hydria

Alabastron

◀ **An *aryballos* and an *alabastron* were flasks used for perfume, perfumed oil and ointments.**

Aryballos

A *loutrophoros* ▶ was a large vase used to bring water for a bride's ceremonial bath (see page 50).

▲
Toilet box called a *pyxis*.

A special type of ▶ *amphora*, filled with oil, was given as a prize at the Panathenaic Games. It was decorated with a picture of the event for which the prize was awarded.

Markets, money and trade

In early times there was no money. People either exchanged goods for other goods of a similar value, or for an agreed amount of metal. Coins were probably invented at the end of the 7th century BC in Lydia, a kingdom in Asia Minor (see page 19). The first coins were made of electrum, a natural mixture of gold and silver.

From Lydia, coins spread to the Ionian Greek colonies and then to the Greek mainland. People soon came to prefer solid gold or silver coins. The Greeks used silver for most of their coins and a round, flat shape soon became standard. It became a sign of a city's independence to issue its own coins. The one exception to this was Sparta, where they continued to use iron rods instead of coins until the 4th century BC.

Greek coins

Early electrum coin from Ionia, marked with parallel lines, c.650-600BC.

Electrum *stater*, a coin from Lydia, showing a lion and a bull, c.561-545BC.

Athenian coin showing an owl (Athene's sacred bird), 5th century BC.

Silver *stater* from Corinth showing Pegasus the winged horse, c.520BC.

The first coins were small lumps of electrum, stamped with official marks to show that their weight and purity were guaranteed by the state.

From 600-480BC animals were the most popular image on coins. They were usually the symbol of the city that issued the coin.

Coin from Katane in Sicily showing Apollo, c.405BC.

Herakles fighting a lion. Silver coin from Herakleia, early 4th century BC.

Gold *stater* from Macedonia depicting Philip II, 359-336BC.

Silver coin from Macedonia, showing Alexander the Great, 336-323BC.

By 480BC, coin-making techniques had greatly improved and the human face and body were shown. Coins usually depicted a god or hero.

In the Hellenistic Period, the quality of the designs on coins declined. One new development was to show portraits of rulers.

Trade

Most trade was done by private merchants who sailed from port to port, buying and selling goods. The states did not normally interfere, except to charge custom duties. There was a great deal of trade between the various states within Greece and with the colonies. The colonies also acted as staging posts for Greek trade with the rest of the world. In the Classical Period, Athens was the leading trading centre, with Corinth a close rival. Each region exported surplus goods or produce. Areas became associated with particular products: for example, Thessaly and Macedonia exported horses, while Athens exported honey and silver. The main Greek exports were oil, wine, pots, statues, metalwork, cloth and books. The main imports are shown on this map.

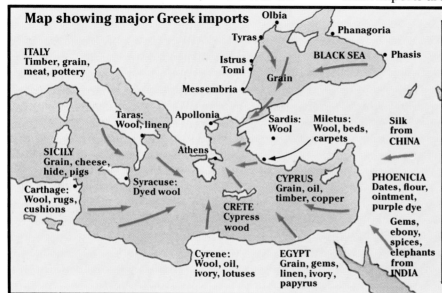

Map showing major Greek imports

Olbia
Tyras
Phanagoria
ITALY Timber, grain, meat, pottery
Istrus
Tomi
BLACK SEA
Phasis
Messembria
Grain
Taras: Wool, linen
Apollonia
Sardis: Wool
Miletus: Wool, beds, carpets
Silk from CHINA
SICILY Grain, cheese, hide, pigs
Athens
Carthage: Wool, rugs, cushions
Syracuse: Dyed wool
CYPRUS Grain, oil, timber, copper
PHOENICIA Dates, flour, ointment, purple dye
CRETE Cypress wood
Gems, ebony, spices, elephants from INDIA
Cyrene: Wool, oil, ivory, lotuses
EGYPT Grain, gems, linen, ivory, papyrus

The grain trade

Grain was the most vital import, as many of the city states could not grow enough of it to feed all their citizens. Athens, for example, had to import two-thirds of the grain it needed. Grain was so important that its trade was controlled by the state, and at one time it was a capital offence to export it. Much of the imported grain came from the Greek colonies around the Black Sea.

Markets

At the heart of every Greek city was the *agora*, or market place. It was the centre of the city's commercial activity, and it was also a social centre where people met their friends. This picture shows what a typical *agora* would have looked like.

This building was called a *stoa*. Shops were often situated behind the row of columns. They were open rooms with a counter across the front, and sold items such as lamps, cooking pots and luxury goods.

People often met their friends in the shade under the colonnades.

Farmers from the surrounding area came to the town to sell their produce. They erected their stalls in the middle of the *agora*. Customers could buy meat, fish, vegetables, cheese, fruit, eggs and hens. Meat and fish sellers often displayed their wares on marble slabs to keep them cool.

Some merchants sold cooked food and drink to the shoppers.

Altar

An *agora* often contained several statues of deities, local athletes and politicians.

Craftsmen usually lived close to the *agora*. They had workshops in their houses where customers went to place special orders. This wall has been cut away to show the inside of a shoe-maker's workshop.

Money changers

Platforms like this one were called *kykloi*. They were used to display goods such as pots, textiles or slaves.

Men who were looking for work gathered in specific areas, where employers could go to hire them. Some of these men were general labourers, but others were professionals, such as cooks or tutors.

Weights and measures

Traders in and around the *agora* were controlled by various officials. In Athens, ten *metronomoi* were chosen annually to check weights and measures. Other officials called *agoranomoi* checked the quality of goods, while *sitophylakes* controlled the grain trade.

This is an official set of weights, against which the seller's weights were checked.

Money changers were known as *trapezitai*, or "table men", because they worked at tables in the agora.

Money changers and bankers

Every city state issued its own coins, so people who wanted to trade with another city had to go to a money changer. They charged a fee for their services and often made so much profit that they were able to lend money. This was the start of banking. A borrower had to pay back his loan by a set date and pay some interest. If he failed to pay he would lose whatever he had pledged to guarantee the loan. This could be his house or his land. People with spare money could also use a banker. He would find a suitable venture to invest it in and would pay the depositor interest from the profits.

Travel by land and sea

As Greece is a very mountainous country, land travel was extremely difficult in ancient times. One of the easiest and quickest ways to travel was by boat. There were many safe harbours and people could pay to travel on one of the merchant ships which sailed around the coast.

Sea travel had its risks too, as dishonest sailors sometimes robbed their passengers once they had put to sea. Ships could also be becalmed or driven off course by the wind. To ensure a safe voyage, a sensible captain always made a sacrifice to the sea god Poseidon before sailing. Ships were also at risk from pirates. It was only in the 5th century BC, when Athenian naval power was at its height, that the Aegean could be successfully policed and the number of pirates was reduced.

Merchant ships

Merchant ships did not normally sail in stormy weather, but even so some were caught and wrecked. Several wrecks have now been located and are being excavated by underwater archaeologists. This reconstruction of a trading ship from about 300BC is based on a wreck discovered off Cyprus.

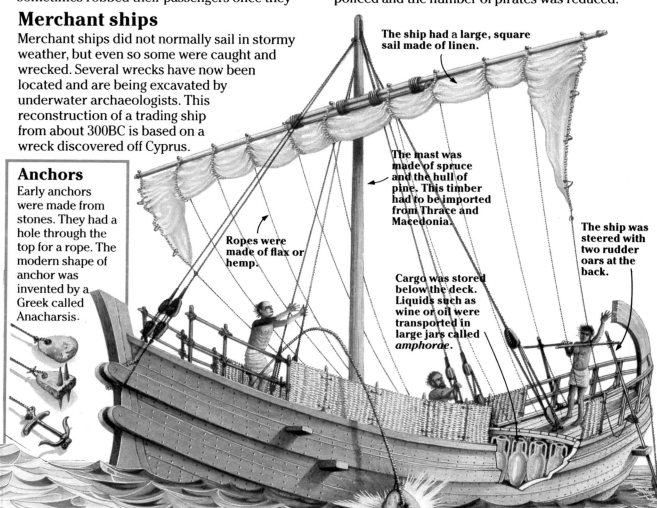

The ship had a large, square sail made of linen.

The mast was made of spruce and the hull of pine. This timber had to be imported from Thrace and Macedonia.

Ropes were made of flax or hemp.

Cargo was stored below the deck. Liquids such as wine or oil were transported in large jars called *amphorae*.

The ship was steered with two rudder oars at the back.

Anchors

Early anchors were made from stones. They had a hole through the top for a rope. The modern shape of anchor was invented by a Greek called Anacharsis.

Navigating techniques

Merchant ships often travelled long distances across open sea, which required great sailing and navigating skills. A Greek called Thales of Miletus studied the Egyptian methods of astronomy and land surveying. He used these to devise a method by which a captain could calculate his distance from land, and a system of navigating by the stars. Anaximander, who lived in the 6th century BC, is said to have been the first person to draw a map of the world. Unfortunately it has not survived.

The kerkouroi

Merchant ships normally relied on sail-power, but writers speak of a ship called a *kerkouroi*, which had both a sail and oars. It had a ram at the front which could be used to fight pirate ships. This picture from a vase painting probably shows a *kerkouroi*.

Greek explorers

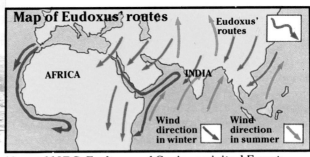

In about 325-300BC, a Greek called Pytheas from Massilia (modern Marseilles) set out to explore northern Europe. He landed in Cornwall and then tried to sail round Britain. After sailing north for six days, he reached another island. Modern scholars are not sure where this was. When he returned home, Pytheas wrote an account of his voyage, but most Greeks did not believe his tales.

About 110BC, Eudoxus of Cyzicus visited Egypt, where he met an Indian sailor. Eudoxus persuaded the man to take him on the trip back to India. He discovered that the monsoon winds carried ships to India from May to September. Then, from November to March, they blew in the other direction and took ships back to Africa. Eudoxus also sailed around the west coast of Africa.

Land travel

Travelling on land was not easy as the country was mountainous and there were few roads. The only good roads led to religious centres such as Eleusis (see page 69). Elsewhere, the roads were often in poor condition and there were hardly any bridges over rivers. Wars between the Greek states meant that people were often forced to make long detours in order to travel in safety.

When most ordinary Greeks went on a journey they had to walk.

Carts were used to transport both people and goods. They could only be used where there was a road, or at least a reasonable surface, to run on.

Rich people often travelled on horseback.

Merchants carrying goods on uneven tracks or over hilly ground used mules and donkeys as pack animals.

Many roads were plagued by bandits who attacked travellers.

Accommodation

Travellers often arranged to stay with relatives or friends along their route. There were inns on the main roads, but many did not provide food, so people had to take supplies with them. In towns, travellers could sleep under the porches of public buildings, but in remote areas they had to sleep in the open.

In some important centres, there were hotels, known as *katagogia*. However, these were often reserved for important visitors. This is a reconstruction of a hotel which has been found at Epidaurus. It had 160 rooms arranged around four courtyards and was two storeys high.

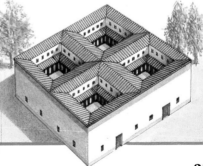

35

The army

At the beginning of the Archaic Period, the most important part of a Greek army was the cavalry. Warriors had to provide their own equipment, so rich aristocrats† came to dominate the army, as they were the only people who could afford a horse and armour. Foot soldiers usually came from the poorer classes, so their weapons and armour were of lower quality.

This statue shows a mounted warrior from the Archaic Period.

Later in the Archaic Period, trade increased, there was more demand for goods, and the middle classes started to prosper. They could now afford good armour and weapons and became heavily armed foot soldiers, known as *hoplites*. By the 7th century BC, foot soldiers were the most important part of the army.

A group of hoplite soldiers

A hoplite's equipment

All hoplites used similar armour and weapons. Most armies did not have a uniform, although in later years some standard elements were adopted to make soldiers recognizable in battle. Spartan hoplites always wore scarlet and the Athenians had shields decorated with the letter "A", for example.

Shields were normally round, and were large enough to protect the body from neck to thigh. They were made of bronze and leather. A hoplite could choose the decoration on his shield and often used a symbol of his family or city. The white legs on this shield were the emblem of the Alcmaeonid family of Athens.

Helmets were made of bronze and often had horsehair crests on top. The shape of helmets changed over the years. Some common styles are shown here.

A hoplite wore a joined breast and back plate, known as a *cuirass*. Early cuirasses were made from two bronze plates, secured with straps at the side. Later, hoplites used a more flexible cuirass, made of leather and bronze.

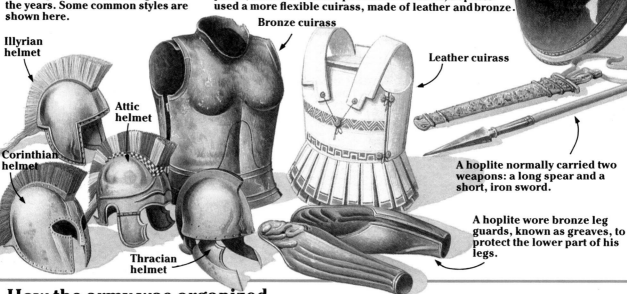

Illyrian helmet

Attic helmet

Corinthian helmet

Thracian helmet

Bronze cuirass

Leather cuirass

A hoplite normally carried two weapons: a long spear and a short, iron sword.

A hoplite wore bronze leg guards, known as greaves, to protect the lower part of his legs.

How the army was organized

Each state had its own procedures for raising and leading its army. In Athens, a man went on to the active service list at 20 and could be called up when there was a war. Men of 50-60 went into the reserve and were used for garrison duties. In an emergency, both young men and veterans might have to fight.

The Athenian forces were led by ten commanders, called *strategoi*, one from each of the Athenian tribes. They were elected by the Assembly. Only one or two *strategoi* were sent out with each military expedition. Each of the ten tribes had to provide enough soldiers for one *phyle*, or regiment, of the army.

In Athens, young men of 18 had to do two years' military training. They were known as *ephebes*.

Battle tactics

As hoplite soldiers began to dominate the Greek armies, new battle tactics were needed and methods of fighting changed completely. In the Bronze Age, warriors had fought individually. Hoplite soldiers, however, fought in organized formations which required good discipline and precise training.

Hoplites fought in a unit known as a phalanx, which was a long block of soldiers, usually eight ranks deep. When a soldier in the front line was killed or injured, his place was taken by the man behind him.

Exposed side

Each hoplite was protected partly by his own shield and partly by his neighbour's. The man on the right-hand end of a line had no neighbour to protect him and was half exposed.

When attacking, a phalanx charged forwards so that the full weight of men and armour smashed into the enemy. If the enemy line did not give way, the two phalanxes had to push until one line broke.

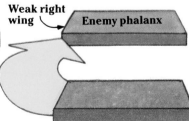

Weak right wing — Enemy phalanx

The right wing of the phalanx was the most vulnerable to attack because the soldiers at this end were partly unprotected. In battle, a general would often try to attack the enemy phalanx on this side.

For the phalanx to be effective, it was important for the men to stay in lines and move as a unit. They used flute music to help them keep in step. This vase painting shows a hoplite phalanx being piped into battle.

Thracian soldiers

In the 5th century BC, the Greeks came into contact with Thracian soldiers, known as *peltasts*. Their tactics were to dash out from cover, hurl javelins into a phalanx and then retreat. When the phalanx formation was broken, the *peltasts* would pick off individual hoplites. To fight them, the Greeks used soldiers known as *ekdromoi*, or "runners out". They were fit, young hoplites, who would run out of the phalanx to chase off the *peltasts*.

A *peltast* carried a small, crescent-shaped wooden shield called a *pelta*.

An *ekdromos* did not use a cuirass or greaves, as these would have weighed him down.

Auxiliary soldiers

Poor men who could not afford the full armour and weapons of a hoplite usually served in lightly armed auxiliary units. These units included archers, stone slingers and soldiers known as *psiloi*, who were armed with clubs and stones.

A *psilos* wore no armour. He used an animal pelt wrapped around his arm to defend himself.

The cavalry

Once hoplites came to dominate the army, the cavalry was much reduced in numbers. By the time of the Persian Wars, the Athenians had only 300 cavalry soldiers. However, horsemen proved to be very useful, both as scouts and to break up an enemy phalanx. The Athenians therefore started to build up their cavalry. By the middle of the 5th century BC they had 1000 cavalrymen.

Each of the ten Athenian tribes was responsible for supplying one squadron of cavalry soldiers. The cavalry was led by two commanders called *hipparchs*, who each controlled five squadrons.

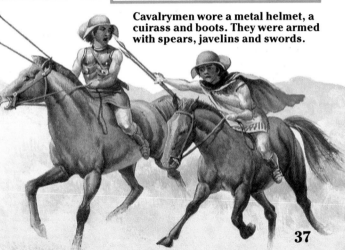

Cavalrymen wore a metal helmet, a cuirass and boots. They were armed with spears, javelins and swords.

Siege warfare

When one Greek state fought another, a common tactic was to lay siege to the enemy city. The army would surround the city and then destroy the enemy's crops, which were usually grown on the plains outside the city. The enemy city would eventually be starved into submission, but this could take a long time.

The besieging army might also try to take the city by force. They used a variety of weapons to attack the city walls and kill the defending soldiers. Some of these devices are shown below.

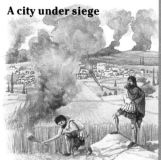

A city under siege

Javelin

The Greeks invented the catapult in the 4th century BC. Early versions were based on the crossbow and ◄ fired arrows or javelins, but later catapults could throw large rocks.

Cauldron containing burning coals, sulphur and pitch.

Hollow tree trunk

Bellows

A flame-thower was sometimes used to destroy wooden walls. Huge bellows pumped air down a hollow tree trunk. This sprayed fire from a cauldron on to the target.

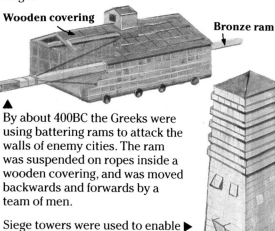

Wooden covering

Bronze ram

▲
By about 400BC the Greeks were using battering rams to attack the walls of enemy cities. The ram was suspended on ropes inside a wooden covering, and was moved backwards and forwards by a team of men.

Siege towers were used to enable ▶ soldiers to climb on to enemy walls. They were sometimes divided into storeys, each of which housed archers or a catapult.

The navy

Whereas Greek merchant ships relied on sails to propel them, their fighting ships had both oars and sails. They could be used simultaneously in open sea, but only the oars were used in a battle.

The more oarsmen a warship had, the faster it could go. At first, oarsmen sat in two rows, one on each side of the ship. Then the Phoenicians invented a ship called a *bireme*, in which the oarsmen on each side of the ship sat in two rows, on two different levels. This doubled the number of oarsmen. In the 6th century BC, the Greeks invented the *trireme*, a ship with three levels of oarsmen on each side.

The trireme

Triremes were fast and easy to manoeuvre. They probably carried crews of up to 200 men, of whom about 170 were rowers. Archaeological evidence from the Athenian dockyard at Piraeus shows that triremes were about 41 metres (135ft) long and 6 metres (20ft) wide. Experts think that in good sea conditions they could reach speeds of around 16 kilometres per hour (10mph).

Triremes had some disadvantages. They were unsafe in stormy sea conditions. There was also no room on board for the crew to cook or sleep, so the ship had to stay close to the coast and land each night. However, they were for many years the most successful warships in the Mediterranean and continued to be used into Roman times.

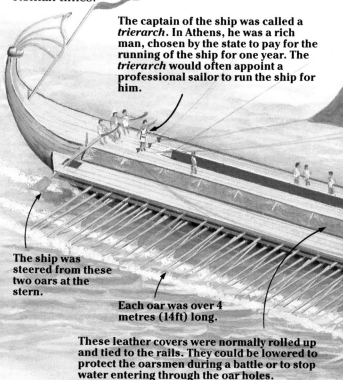

The captain of the ship was called a *trierarch*. In Athens, he was a rich man, chosen by the state to pay for the running of the ship for one year. The *trierarch* would often appoint a professional sailor to run the ship for him.

The ship was steered from these two oars at the stern.

Each oar was over 4 metres (14ft) long.

These leather covers were normally rolled up and tied to the rails. They could be lowered to protect the oarsmen during a battle or to stop water entering through the oar holes.

Early ships

In the Archaic Period, the standard Greek warship was a *pentecounter*. It had 50 oarsmen. Some experts believe that the oars were in a straight line, others think that the oarsmen sat on two levels.

By the 8th century BC, the Phoenicians were using a warship called a *bireme*. It had two rows of oars on each side of the ship and a raised deck which carried archers and warriors.

The oarsmen

Greek oarsmen were free men and professional sailors, who were usually recruited from the poorer classes. We do not know exactly how the three rows of oarsmen were arranged on a trireme. Three possible seating plans are shown here. Experts now think that the first arrangement was most likely.

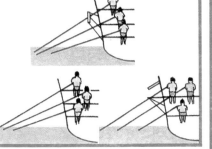

Battle tactics

At the time of the Persian Wars, trireme tactics were to row hard and ram the enemy ship. This would sink or at least incapacitate it. The Greek troops then fired arrows at the enemy crew. If necessary, they boarded the enemy ship and defeated any remaining crew in hand-to-hand fighting.

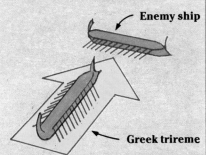

Enemy ship

Greek trireme

As triremes became swifter and lighter, tactics changed. A trireme would row towards an enemy ship, but swerve away at the last moment. The rowers pulled their oars on board and the trireme glided past the enemy ship, breaking its oars. The disabled ship could then be rammed and boarded easily.

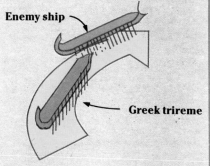

Enemy ship

Greek trireme

The mast was usually made of a wood called spruce. The wood was specially imported from Thrace and Macedonia. The mast was lowered on to the deck before a battle.

The sail was probably made of linen. It was used when the trireme was in open sea, but was lowered before a battle. The ship was more stable and easier to manoeuvre when the sail and mast were lowered.

A trireme carried a number of archers and soldiers, who travelled on the upper deck. In a battle they fired at the enemy crew and tried to board their ship.

The prow of the ship was equipped with a bronze ram, which was used to sink enemy ships. The whole prow area was heavily reinforced, sometimes with metal. The front of the ship was often decorated with a painted eye to scare the enemy.

The Persian Wars

In the 6th century BC, the Greeks were threatened by a people called the Persians, who came from the area that is now Iran (see page opposite). As the Persians expanded their empire westwards, they tried to seize Greek territory. In 546BC, they conquered the Ionian states on the west coast of Asia Minor. In 500-499BC the Ionians became discontented with Persian rule and rebelled, helped by a naval force from Athens and Eretria. The Ionians were successful at first, but the Persians eventually crushed the revolt. This was the start of a series of wars between the Greeks and the Persians, which lasted from 490-449BC.

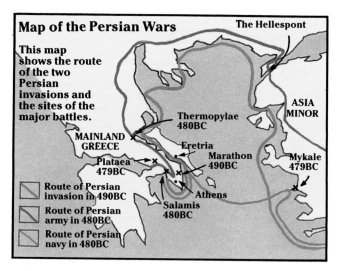

Map of the Persian Wars

This map shows the route of the two Persian invasions and the sites of the major battles.

- The Hellespont
- ASIA MINOR
- Thermopylae 480BC
- MAINLAND GREECE
- Eretria
- Marathon 490BC
- Mykale 479BC
- Plataea 479BC
- Athens
- Salamis 480BC

Route of Persian invasion in 490BC
Route of Persian army in 480BC
Route of Persian navy in 480BC

The Battle of Marathon

The Persians did not forgive Athens and Eretria for helping the Ionians. In 490BC, led by King Darius, they crushed Eretria. Then they landed at Marathon, a place on the coast north east of Athens. The Athenians and their allies raised an army of 10,000 troops, led by a general called Miltiades†. Although the Greeks were heavily outnumbered by the Persians, they won the battle. This was due to Miltiades' superior military tactics and the strength of the hoplite† phalanx (see page 37).

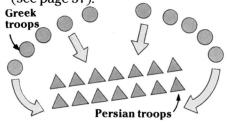

Greek troops

Persian troops

The Greeks concentrated their troops on the wings. They were able to attack the Persians at the sides and then from behind.

The second Persian invasion

Many Greeks thought that the Persians would invade again. A politician called Themistocles† persuaded the Athenians to improve their city's defences by building up its navy. In 480BC the Persians did invade, led by King Xerxes. Many of the Greek states joined forces to fight the Persians.

The Athenians consulted the Oracle† at Delphi (see page 68) and were told that Athens would be saved by a wooden wall. Some Athenians believed the Oracle was describing the wooden city walls, but Themistocles convinced them that the message in fact referred to the wooden ships in the city's navy. He therefore prepared for a naval battle.

In 480BC the Persians crossed the Hellespont (see map) on a bridge made of boats. Their huge army was said to have taken seven days to march across.

The Battle of Thermopylae

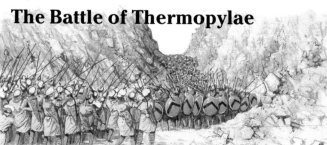

The first battle between the Greeks and Xerxes' army took place in 480BC in a narrow mountain pass called Thermopylae. A small army of Spartans and Boeotians, led by King Leonidas, were able to prevent the Persians getting through. However, a Greek traitor showed some of the Persians another route around the pass. Leonidas knew he would be surrounded and sent most of his soldiers away to safety. He fought on with just a few troops. They were hopelessly outnumbered and were all killed.

The destruction of Athens

After Thermopylae, the Persians marched south to attack Athens. The Athenian leader, Themistocles, was still determined to fight the Persians at sea, so he withdrew most of his troops and allowed the Persians to seize the city. They murdered the few defending Athenians, burned the temples on the Acropolis† and plundered the city.

The Battles of Salamis and Plataea

The Persians also sent a naval force to attack the Greeks. There was a decisive sea battle in 480BC around the island of Salamis, off the coast of Athens. Themistocles lured the Persian fleet into the channel of water between Salamis and the mainland. There the Greek navy took them by surprise. The Persian ships were unable to manoeuvre in the narrow waters and after a fierce battle they were defeated.

The Battle of Salamis

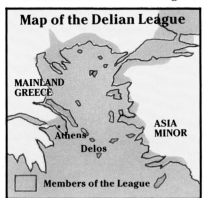

In 479BC the Greeks assembled an enormous army, led by the Spartan general, Pausanias, and defeated the Persian army at a place called Plataea. At the same time the Greek navy attacked and burned the Persian fleet, while it was beached at Mykale on the coast of Asia Minor. This marked the end of the Persian invasion.

The Delian League

Many Greeks believed that it was only a matter of time before the Persians tried to avenge their defeat. In order to be ready for this, many of the Greek states formed a league, led by Athens.

Map of the Delian League

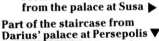

MAINLAND GREECE

Athens
Delos

ASIA MINOR

Members of the League

Members of the league contributed ships and money to provide a navy to defend them. It is known as the Delian League, as it first met in 478BC on the island of Delos, where the common treasury was kept.

The end of the Persian Wars

Although the Greeks had succeeded in stopping the Persian invasion of mainland Greece, the wars did not come to an abrupt end. The Greeks and Persians continued to fight over various territories around the Mediterranean, such as Egypt, Cyprus and Ionia. In 449BC the Delian League signed a peace treaty with Persia, but most Greeks continued to dislike and fear the Persians.

The Persians

Map of the Persian Empire c.485BC

GREECE
LYDIA
• Sardis
IONIA
ASSYRIA
MEDIA
Susa
• Persepolis
PERSIA
EGYPT

Original Persian territory

Extent of empire under Darius I

The Persians came from the area now called Iran. In 550BC they conquered the neighbouring kingdom of Media and started to expand their territory, eventually acquiring an enormous empire. Their empire was divided into 20 provinces, each governed by an official called a *satrap*. A system of roads made communication between the king and the provinces easy.

The Persians owed their success to an extremely efficient army. Most of their troops were Persian, and there was an elite force of 10,000 warriors, known as the Immortals.

Picture of two Immortals from the palace at Susa ▶

Part of the staircase from Darius' palace at Persepolis ▼

Key dates

550BC King Cyrus II of Persia defeats the Medes and founds the Achaemenid dynasty.

522-485BC Reign of the Persian King, Darius I. The Persian Empire reaches its largest extent (see map above).

500-499BC The Greek colonies in Ionia revolt against the Persians, but are defeated.

490BC First Persian invasion of Greece. The Persians are defeated at the Battle of Marathon.

480BC Second Persian invasion of Greece; Battle of Thermopylae; destruction of Athens; naval Battle of Salamis.

479BC Battle of Plataea; the Greeks defeat the Persian invasion.

465-330BC Persian Empire declines and is eventually conquered by Alexander the Great† (see pages 74-75).

The city of Athens

Athens is dominated by a rocky hill called the *Acropolis*, which means "high city" in Greek. People settled there from the earliest times because it had a spring of water and was easy to defend. In Mycenaean times there was a small city on the Acropolis, surrounded by stone walls.

By the end of the Dark Ages, the Acropolis had become a sacred place used only for temples and shrines. Other public buildings and people's houses were built around the base of the hill.

In 480BC Athens was sacked by the Persians (see page 40) and the temples on the Acropolis were destroyed. A few years later, a massive rebuilding programme was launched by the politician, Pericles†. The temples which still stand on the Acropolis were built at this time.

By the Classical Period, there were probably over 250,000 people living in Athens and the surrounding countryside. The city had its own port on the coast at Piraeus, about six kilometres (four miles) away. This reconstruction shows what the city of Athens probably looked like at the end of the Classical Period.

The Acropolis

This temple, called the *Erechtheum*, was built in 421-406BC. It was constructed on the site of the contest between Poseidon and Athene (see right) and a sacred olive tree grew in its courtyard. The temple was named after Erechtheus, who was the legendary ancestor of the city's Mycenaean kings. It contained a wooden statue of Athene, which the Greeks believed had fallen to earth in ancient times.

This huge, bronze statue of *Athene Promachos* (Athene the Champion) was made by the sculptor Pheidias†. On clear days, it could be seen by sailors returning to the port at Piraeus.

This gateway leading to the sacred enclosure was called the *Propylaea*. It was built in 437-432BC by the architect Mnesicles.

The temple of *Athene Nike* (Athene the Victorious) was built in 426BC by the architect Callicrates.

City walls

The *Agora*† was the market place and the centre of the town. It was surrounded by long colonnades called *stoa*† which contained shops.

This building, called the *Tholos*, was used by the leaders of the Council.

The city council held its meetings in this building, called the *Bouleuterion*.

This road led to the *Dipylon Gate*, which was one of the main entrances to the city.

This temple was dedicated to Hephaestos, the god of blacksmiths and craftsmen. It is also known as the *Theseum*, after the Athenian hero Theseus.

The *Parthenon* was built between 447-438BC by the architect Ictinus. It was a temple to the goddess Athene, who was the patron goddess of the city. Athens was named after her.

Altar

This concert hall, called the *Odeon*, was used for contests of music and poetry.

A drama festival was held in this theatre each year in honour of the god Dionysus.

Acropolis

The *Panathenaic Way* was the main road to the Acropolis. It was the route used by a special procession, which took place every four years in honour of Athene.

The Court of Justice was situated on this hill, called the *Areopagus*. It was named after the god Ares who, according to legend, once stood trial here for murder.

Houses near the *agora* were often occupied by craftsmen. Many blacksmiths' forges were situated close to the temple of Hephaestos.

The Assembly of Athenian citizens met on this hill, called the *Pnyx*, to take decisions on the government of the city.

The naming of Athens

According to legend, the gods Athene and Poseidon quarrelled over the naming of the greatest town in Greece. Poseidon thrust his trident into a rock on the Acropolis. Sea water gushed out, and Poseidon promised the people riches through sea trade if they named the city after him.

Athene planted an olive tree as her gift to the people. It was decided that she had given the more valuable gift and the city was called Athens in her honour. Athene's sacred olive tree was burnt when the city was sacked by the Persians, but when it later threw out green shoots it brought new hope to the Athenians.

The return of Theseus

Theseus was a legendary king (see page 82), said to have ruled Athens in the Mycenaean Age. At the Battle of Marathon in 490BC, the spirit of Theseus was said to have charged towards the Persian ranks, inspiring the Athenians to victory.

After this the Oracle of Delphi (see page 68) ordered that Theseus' bones should be brought back to Athens from the island of Skyros, where he had died. On the island, the Athenians saw an eagle tearing at the ground. They dug in this spot and discovered a coffin containing bones and bronze armour. They knew this must be Theseus, and reburied him in Athens.

43

Architecture

The Greeks attached little importance to the building of private houses, which were usually simple structures made of mud and brick. Instead, they devoted their money and skills to public buildings. The most important of these were temples, which provided a focus for both civic pride and religious feelings. In the Classical Period, the city state was therefore the most important patron for architects, sculptors and painters.

Building materials and techniques

From the 7th century BC, temples and other large, public buildings were made of stone. Limestone or marble were the normal materials, but in the western colonies sandstone was also used. Parts of the building, such as the roof frame and ceilings, were built from wood. Roof tiles were usually made of terracotta†, although some great temples had stone tiles. This scene shows how a temple was constructed.

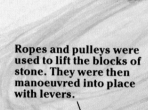

Blocks of stone were brought from the quarry on wagons.

Each block was joined to the ones beside it with pieces of metal called cramps, and joined to the ones above and below with rods called dowels.

Cramp

Blocks were shaped on the ground. Masons used hammers, mallets and various kinds of chisel to shape the stone.

Ropes and pulleys were used to lift the blocks of stone. They were then manoeuvred into place with levers.

Columns were made from a number of cylindrical pieces of stone, called drums, held together with metal pegs.

The grooves on the pillars, known as fluting, were started when the drums were on the ground and completed when the columns had been erected.

When they were in place, the stones were polished with a hard stone and a lubricant.

Public buildings

▲
A *tholos* was a round building with a conical roof, surrounded by columns. The *tholos* in Athens was used as a meeting place for members of the city's council. This reconstruction shows the *tholos* in Delphi, which was probably used for religious purposes.

A *stoa* was a building with a row of columns at the front. It was used to provide shelter from the sun and rain. *Stoas* were often built round an agora and often contained shops or offices behind the colonnade.
▼

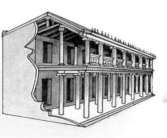

Treasuries were built at religious centres to house the offerings made by a *polis*† and its citizens. They resembled small temples, and consisted of a single room with a porch in front. This is the Athenian treasury at Delphi.
▼

▲
Altars were erected in the open air, often in front of a temple entrance. They were usually just a slab of stone, but some could be very large and ornate. This reconstruction shows the altar of Zeus and Athene at Pergamum, which was built in the Hellenistic Period by King Eumenes II.

Architectural styles

The design of most Greek buildings was based on a series of vertical pillars with horizontal lintels. This style probably came from earlier buildings in which tree trunks were used to support the roof. The proportions, such as the number and height of the pillars and the distance between them, were carefully calculated to achieve a balanced effect. In the architecture of temples, two main styles, or orders, emerged. They are known as the Doric and the Ionic Orders.

The Doric Order

This style was popular in mainland Greece. It was a simple style with sturdy columns whose tops, or capitals, were undecorated.

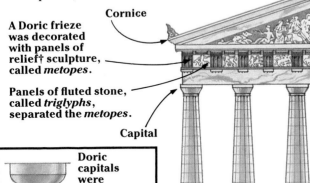

A Doric frieze was decorated with panels of relief† sculpture, called *metopes*.

Cornice

Panels of fluted stone, called *triglyphs*, separated the *metopes*.

Capital

Doric capitals were undecorated.

The Ionic Order

The Ionic style was popular in the eastern colonies and on the islands. It was a more elegant style than the Doric, and had thinner columns with decorated capitals.

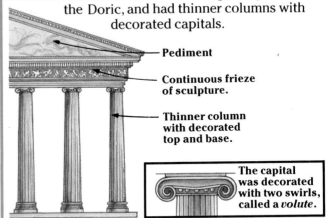

Pediment

Continuous frieze of sculpture.

Thinner column with decorated top and base.

The capital was decorated with two swirls, called a *volute*.

Other column styles

An early form of the Ionic column has been found at Smyrna and on Lesbos. This style is known as Aeolic. It is thought to date from the 6th century BC.

The Corinthian column was a later variation of the Ionic. It had an elaborate capital, decorated with acanthus leaves. The Greeks did not often use Corinthian columns, but they became very popular in Roman times.

Sometimes a statue of a girl, called a *caryatid*, was used as a column. The most famous *caryatids* are in the *Erechtheum* on the Acropolis in Athens.

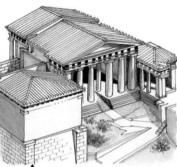

A votive monument was one erected in honour of a hero, or of a great victory in an athletic competition, a festival or a war. This lion was built as a memorial to the Theban soldiers who fought in the Battle of Chaeronea in 338BC. ▼

▲ A *propylaea* was an elaborate gateway, which formed the entrance to the sacred enclosure at a religious sanctuary. The most famous *propylaea* is the one on the Acropolis in Athens which was built in 437-432BC.

Decoration of buildings

The statues, friezes and sometimes also the walls of public buildings were painted. Fragments from early mural paintings show that a flat, two-dimensional style was used. In the Classical Period a more realistic style was introduced, and the Greeks became the first people to make use of perspective in their pictures. In the Hellenistic Period, wealthy people often had their houses decorated with murals.

Very few Greek murals have survived. However, this painting from Pompeii in Italy was probably painted by a Greek artist.

Sculpture

The Greeks made large numbers of statues, as they used them for a wide variety of purposes. Sculptures were used to decorate temples and people's homes, to commemorate famous people and to mark graves. Although some Greek statues have been lost, others have been preserved, sometimes in rather unusual ways. For example, the remains of many broken statues have been discovered on the Acropolis† in Athens, where they were buried after the city had been sacked by the Persians in 480BC (see page 40). Other statues, which were lost in shipwrecks, have recently been recovered from the sea. Many Roman copies of famous Greek statues have also survived although the originals have been lost.

Stone statues

Sculptors used a chisel and mallet to carve the stone.

Clothes were painted in bright colours, such as red or blue.

Hair was painted yellow.

Stone statues were made from limestone or marble. As large blocks of stone were difficult to transport, they were usually cut in the quarry to the rough shape of the statue. The more detailed carving was done later in a workshop, like the one shown here.

Finished statues were originally painted, but most of the paint has now worn away. Sometimes inlaid glass, coloured stone or ivory was used for the eyes. Details such as weapons, crowns, jewellery or horses' tackle were made of bronze fitted on to the stone.

Terracotta

Terracotta is a mixture of clay and sand which was used to make small statues and plaques for temples. Small figures illustrating scenes from daily life were also made of terracotta. This one from the 6th century BC shows a barber at work.

Wood

◄ In early times, statues were probably made of wood, but as it decays quickly few of them have survived. This rare wooden statue showing Zeus and Hera was made in c.625-600BC.

Bronze

The Greeks also made many bronze statues, but only a few of them have survived. Some of these are shown on page 48.

Styles of sculpture

The Archaic Period: c.800-480BC

At first statues were only made in a ► limited number of poses, which were copied from Egyptian art. Normally the figure was standing in a very stiff, formal position, with its left leg forward and arms at its side. Its facial expression was always a half-smile.

The Classical Period: c.480-323BC

In this period, it ► was fashionable for sculptors to portray deities or god-like men and women, with detached and serene facial expressions. This is a Roman copy of a statue by Praxiteles†, c.350-330BC.

Sculptors liked to show figures in the middle of an action. This discus thrower is ◄ a Roman copy of a statue made by the sculptor Myron† in c.460-450BC.

The Hellenistic Period: c.323-100BC

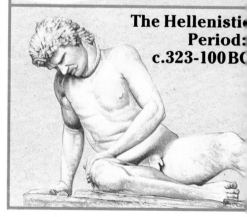

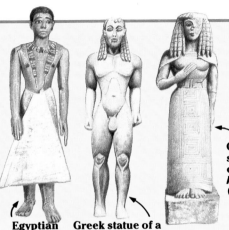

Egyptian statue

Greek statue of a young man, called a _kouros_ (youth).

Greek statue of a _kore_ (maiden).

Greek artists soon became dissatisfied with this formal approach and began experimenting with relaxed and supple figures and more adventurous poses. This statue of an archer was made in c.500-480BC. ▼

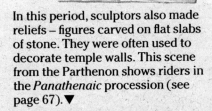

Sculptors also started to show the folds of material in clothes. At first these were just rigid lines, but they became more realistic, as shown on this figure of a goddess made in c.480BC. ►

As sculptors became more skilled at showing facial expressions, they began to produce portraits of famous people. This is the Athenian leader, Pericles (see page 62). ►

In this period, sculptors also made reliefs – figures carved on flat slabs of stone. They were often used to decorate temple walls. This scene from the Parthenon shows riders in the _Panathenaic_ procession (see page 67). ▼

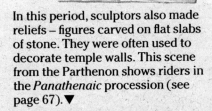

Athens was a famous centre for carving gravestones. This gravestone for a woman called Hegeso was made in c.400BC. ▼

◄ There was also a growing interest in portraying the female body. The first known female nude is this statue of Aphrodite by Praxiteles, made c.350-330BC.

◄ Sculptors also produced special reliefs which people left in temples to thank the gods for favours. This one was dedicated to Asclepius, the god of medicine.

In the 4th century BC sculptors ► became more interested in human qualities. Facial expressions on statues were often gentle and tender. This Roman copy shows the mythical characters, Eirene and Ploutos, by the sculptor Kephisodotos.

In the Hellenistic Period, sculptors started to portray a wider range of characters. Old age, childhood, pain and even death were now acceptable subjects. This is a Roman copy of a ◄ statue showing a dying man.

Physical deformities were also shown. This boxer with battered features is a typical example of the new subject matter in the Hellenistic Period. ◄

Hellenistic sculptures ► could be highly dramatic. This Roman copy shows a man killing himself and his wife.

Metalworkers and miners

During the Mycenaean period the principal metal used for weapons and tools was bronze. Iron was introduced during the Dark Ages, but it was only used for a limited range of objects and many things continued to be produced in bronze. Gold and silver were always used for luxury items.

In Athens, the metalworkers had their own quarter near the temple of Hephaestos, who was their patron deity. Most smiths worked in small workshops in their homes.

Bronze

Bronze is an alloy which is made by adding a small amount of tin to copper. The Greeks imported copper from Cyprus and the eastern Mediterranean and tin from Spain, Brittany and even Cornwall. They used bronze to make a wide variety of objects, some of which are shown below. As bronze was a valuable metal, it was often melted down and re-used, so few large items have survived.

Bronze was a favourite material for statues. Some of the statues we have were originally lost at sea in shipwrecks and have only recently been found by underwater archaeologists.

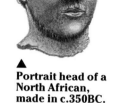

This statue ▶ probably represents the god Poseidon throwing a trident. It was made in c.470-450BC and was found in the sea off Cape Sounion, near Athens.

▲ A boy jockey and his horse, made in c.330-310BC. This statue was probably a victory monument from the Olympic Games.

▲ Portrait head of a North African, made in c.350BC.

◀ Armour was usually made of bronze (see page 36). This vase painting shows an armourer at work on a helmet.

Bronze was used to make household articles, such as vases, mirrors and kitchen utensils. This bronze mirror from Athens was ◀ made in c.500BC.

◀ This enormous bronze *krater* was discovered at Vix in France. It is 1.64 metres (5.4ft) high, weighs 208 kilos (458lb) and holds about 1200 litres (317 gallons).

Methods of working bronze

Hammering

The earliest bronze statues were made from sheets of bronze hammered and riveted over a wooden core.

Casting

Later, small statues were made of solid metal, cast in moulds.

The lost wax method

Not all statues were solid metal. Some were made by the lost wax method, shown below. Large statues were made in sections and joined together.

1 Clay core   Wax model built around core.

First a clay core was made and pins were stuck in it. The statue was modelled in wax around the core.

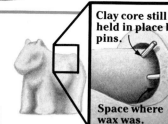

Clay core still held in place by pins.

Space where wax was.

2

The model was covered with more clay and heated. The wax melted and then ran out, leaving a space.

Finished statue

3

Molten bronze could then be poured into the gap. When the bronze had set, the clay mould was removed.

Iron

Iron was first used in Greece in about 1050BC and steadily increased in importance. Iron was used principally for tools and weapons, as it could be made sharper and harder than bronze.

The use of iron required the invention of new technology. In bronze-making, the furnace only needed to be heated to around 1090°C (1994°F), but to work iron a much higher temperature was required.

This reconstruction of an iron furnace is based on one shown on a vase painting. When the furnace was heated, the molten iron gathered at the bottom and could be removed with tongs.

The furnace was built of brick and lined with clay to retain the heat.

One man pumped these goatskin bellows to increase the temperature in the furnace.

Layers of charcoal and iron ore were placed in here.

Iron from the furnace had to be hammered while it was still red hot to remove impurities.

Special tongs were used to move the hot metal.

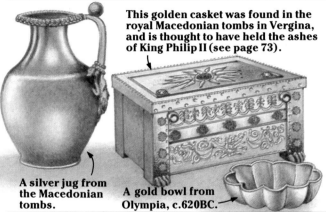

This golden casket was found in the royal Macedonian tombs in Vergina, and is thought to have held the ashes of King Philip II (see page 73).

A silver jug from the Macedonian tombs.

A gold bowl from Olympia, c.620BC.

Gold and silver

Precious metals were used to make coins, jewellery and luxury goods. We also know of several large statues made of gold and ivory, such as the statue of Athene in the Parthenon (see page 66). Few gold and silver items from Ancient Greece have survived, as they were often melted down so that the metal could be re-used. In addition, they were often stolen by tomb robbers or conquerors. When the Romans occupied Greece in the 2nd century BC, they stole huge numbers of gold and silver objects.

Silver mining

Most of the Greeks' silver came from the mines at Laurion near Athens. These mines were worked from at least the 8th century BC.

The mines were owned by the Athenian state, but they were leased out to private contractors. The mining itself was done by slaves, who were hired by the contractors from their owners. By the 5th century BC there were as many as 20,000 slaves working at Laurion. Conditions were grim, with miners working shifts of up to ten hours. This reconstruction of a mine shows how the ore was extracted.

Narrow galleries fanned out into the seams of silver ore. In some places miners had to crawl along them and then lie on their backs to work.

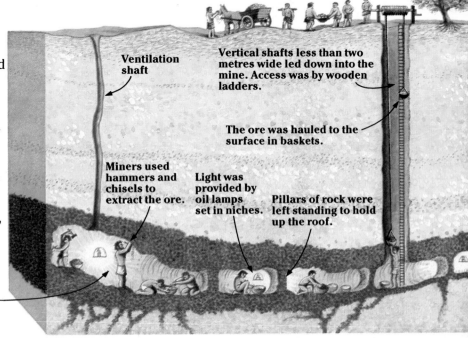

Ventilation shaft

Vertical shafts less than two metres wide led down into the mine. Access was by wooden ladders.

The ore was hauled to the surface in baskets.

Miners used hammers and chisels to extract the ore.

Light was provided by oil lamps set in niches.

Pillars of rock were left standing to hold up the roof.

The role of women

Women in most states in ancient Greece led very sheltered lives and were not permitted to play an active role in society. They could not take part in the running of the city. They were not allowed to inherit or own property, or to conduct any legal transaction. They could not even buy anything that cost over a certain amount of money. Throughout their lives they were always under the control of a male relative: first their father, then their husband, brother or son.

Marriage

A girl was only about 15 when she was married, but the bridegroom was likely to be much older. Plato said that 30-35 was the best age for a man to marry. A girl's father chose her husband and provided her with money and goods, called a dowry. This was administered by her husband, but would return to her father if she were divorced or left a widow without children.

Loutrophorus

On the day before her wedding a bride sacrificed her toys to the goddess Artemis, as a sign that her childhood was ending. She bathed in water from a sacred spring, brought in a vase called a *loutrophorus*.

Servants dressing the bride

On the wedding day, the bride wore white. Both families made sacrifices and feasted. In the evening, the bridegroom went to the bride's house. This was often the first time that the bride and groom met.

The bride and groom then rode to his house, in a chariot if they were rich, or a cart if they were not. They were accompanied by a procession, led by torch bearers and musicians.

They were met at the door by the groom's mother. The bride was carried over the threshold and then led to the family hearth to join the religious life of her new family.

The bride and groom shared some food before the hearth as a symbol of their union. Then they were showered with nuts, fruits and sweets to bring them luck and prosperity.

Finally the bride was led to the bedroom, amidst much laughing and joking. On the following day both families met at the husband's house for a party and presents were given.

A wife's duties

In a wealthy household, a bride had many duties. Each day she inspected the stores, and ensured that the house was clean and tidy and that meals were ready on time. She looked after the children and any sick members of the household, and managed the family finances.

The women of the household produced all the cloth needed for clothes and furnishings. Spinning and weaving therefore occupied a large amount of a wife's time. This reconstruction, based on a 6th century vase painting, shows a wife supervising the various stages involved in making cloth.

The mistress of the household would have been seated. Here she is preparing some wool for spinning and supervising the work.

These women are weighing bales of wool on a pair of scales.

This woman is spinning the wool. She holds the wool on a distaff and uses a spindle to stretch out the thread.

The thread is woven into cloth on a loom.

These women are folding the finished piece of cloth.

Social life

The slave carried a parasol to protect the lady from the sun.

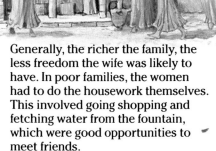

In Athens, married women from good families did not often leave the house. They normally went out only for religious festivals and family celebrations, or to do small bits of personal shopping. Whenever they went out, they were accompanied by a slave.

Sometimes they were allowed to visit their women friends. This terracotta† shows two ladies chatting. Women also gave dinner parties for their female friends, but we know little about them. Men and women only mixed at strictly family parties.

Generally, the richer the family, the less freedom the wife was likely to have. In poor families, the women had to do the housework themselves. This involved going shopping and fetching water from the fountain, which were good opportunities to meet friends.

Divorce

A woman had to be virtuous and absolutely faithful to her husband. She would be divorced and lose her dowry if he suspected that she were not.

If a man wanted to divorce his wife, he just made a formal statement of divorce in front of witnesses. It was much more difficult for a woman to end an unhappy marriage, because she could not take legal action herself. She had to go to an official called an *archon* (see page 61) and persuade him to act on her behalf.

In a divorce, the husband kept the children and sent his wife back to her nearest male relative.

Hetairai

Hetairai were invited to men's dinner parties. They were trained to join in the conversation.

Not every girl was brought up to be a virtuous wife. Some girls, usually from the lower classes or foreigners, would become *hetairai*, or companions. They had to be pretty and clever, and were carefully trained to be skilled musicians and witty, interesting speakers. They took wealthy lovers who could support them in comfort.

Beauty

Oil bottles in the shape of feet.

Greek ladies spent a lot of time, effort and money on making themselves beautiful. It became the custom to have a bath every day. After the bath, perfumed oil was rubbed into the skin to prevent the drying effect of the sun.

This vase painting shows a woman washing her hair. Oil was also used on the hair to make it shine. Some women dyed their hair or used wigs. Others used padding to improve their figure, or wore thick-soled sandals to make themselves taller.

Many women wore make-up. They used rouge to make their cheeks pink and darkened their eyebrows. It was fashionable for the skin to be pale and make-up was used to make the skin white. This vase painting shows a woman admiring herself in a mirror.

Childhood and education

Greek citizens were taught that it was their patriotic duty to get married and father sons. In Sparta, for example, penalties were imposed on men who stayed single for too long. The State encouraged people to have sons to provide future citizens and soldiers.

Parents also benefited from having a son, as it ensured that there would be someone to support them in their old age. Daughters could not do this because they were not permitted to inherit property or money. If a man did not have a son, he could adopt a boy who would inherit from him.

Babies

Cot

Baby's feeding bottle

Potty

When a baby was born, the mother presented it to her husband. If he did not believe that it was his child, or if the baby was handicapped, he could reject it. The baby would then be abandoned and left to die. Baby girls were most often rejected.

People who did not want another child, or who could not afford to raise one, might also abandon their babies. In some states unwanted babies were left in a specific place. People could go there, adopt a child and bring it up to be their slave.

A family who could afford it would hire a poor neighbour or a slave as a nurse for the baby. Wealthy families would also have special furniture made for their children, some of which has been found on the sites of excavated houses.

Seven days after the birth of a baby, the front door of the house was decorated with olive garlands for a boy or woollen ones for a girl. The family would make a sacrifice to the gods and a party was held for all the relatives, who brought gifts.

During the celebrations, a ceremony called the *amphidromia* took place. The women of the house carried the baby round the hearth to bring it into the religious life of the family. The baby was named at this ceremony or on the tenth day of its life.

At the age of three, a child's infancy was considered to be over. In Athens this was marked at the *Anthesteria* festival (see page 67). On the second day of the festival, children aged three were presented with small jugs like the one shown above.

Education in Sparta

Spartan schooling emphasized physical fitness. The most important subjects were athletics, dancing and weapon training. Pupils were also taught music and patriotic songs, Spartan law and some poetry. However, these more academic subjects were not considered important, as the aim of the Spartan system was to produce tough, healthy adults who would become warriors and mothers of warriors.

At seven, a boy was sent to live in a barracks, supervised by a teacher called a *paidonome*.

Each boy was allotted to a group, and several groups made up a class. The boys elected leaders, who helped to organize the work.

Boys had to make their own beds from rushes and they were not allowed to have covers.

Each boy was given one tunic to wear throughout the year. From the age of 12 boys also went bare-headed and bare-footed.

School

Greek education aimed to produce good citizens who could participate fully in the running of their state. Physical fitness was considered to be as important as learning. A boy's education usually began at the age of seven, and could go on until he started his military training at 18 (see page 36). As education had to be paid for, it is unlikely that the children of the poorer citizens received more than a very basic schooling. Girls did not go to school and were usually taught by their mothers at home. A rich family often hired a slave called a *paidagogos* to supervise their son's schooling. He escorted the boy to school and stayed during the classes to keep an eye on the boy's behaviour.

Wax covered tablet

Grammatistes *Paidagogos*

A boy attended three schools. The first was run by a teacher called a *grammatistes*, who taught reading, writing and arithmetic. Each pupil wrote with a stylus on wooden tablets covered in wax. They used pebbles or an abacus to do sums.

Poems were written on scrolls of papyrus.

A boy was taught music and poetry by a teacher called a *kitharistes*. He was taught to play the lyre and the pipes. He also had to learn extracts of poetry by heart, as an educated man was expected to quote the great poets in his conversation.

The third type of school was run by a *paidotribes*, who taught dancing and athletics. He probably took his pupils to a *gymnasium*† (a training ground) or a *palaistra* (a wrestling school) to practise. His pupils could take part in competitive games (see page 58).

Higher education

There was no formal higher education, but from the 5th century BC teachers called *sophists* travelled from place to place instructing young men in the art of public speaking. Philosophers like Socrates† often taught informally at a *gymnasium* and attracted groups of devoted young followers. In the 4th century BC, Plato†, Aristotle† and others set up permanent schools at *gymnasia* in Athens. By the Hellenistic Period, it was common for *gymnasia* to provide lecture rooms and libraries as part of their facilities.

Philosophers taught their pupils under the colonnades or in the dressing rooms at a *gymnasium*. They discussed subjects such as mathematics, science, politics and history.

The food was inadequate and the boys were encouraged to steal extra food from local farms.

Once a year there was a competition in which the boys were beaten to see who could bear the most pain without complaining. Some boys died during the thrashing.

Boys bathed in the river.

Boys were allowed to attend the men's meals in the barracks. They listened and took part in the discussions, but absolute respect and obedience to their elders was expected.

Spartan girls were also educated in order to produce physically fit and disciplined women. They were trained in gymnastics, music, singing and dancing, and took part in athletic competitions. This picture shows a Spartan dancing class.

Music and poetry

Music was very important in the daily lives of the Greeks. There were songs and music for most social events: songs to celebrate a birth or lament a death, drinking songs and love songs. There were work-songs for farmers, and warriors and athletes trained to the sound of pipe music. Music was also used to accompany poetry, and as part of religious festivals and theatrical performances (see page 56).

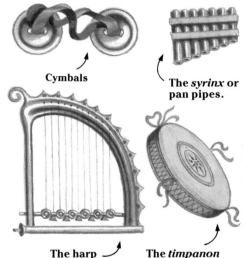

The sons and daughters of citizens were usually taught music. This vase painting shows a child being taught to play the *auloi* (see below).

Musical instruments

We do not know what Greek music sounded like because it was not normally written down. Only some small fragments of pieces of music have been found and it is difficult to interpret what the symbols mean. However, we do know what Greek musical instruments looked like because they were often depicted on vases and in paintings. Some common instruments are shown here.

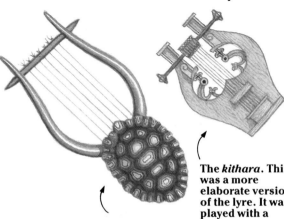

The lyre. According to legend, the lyre was invented by the god Hermes. He made it from the shell of a tortoise and the hide and horns of an ox he had stolen.

The *kithara*. This was a more elaborate version of the lyre. It was played with a plectrum and tended to be used in musical contests and by professional musicians.

Cymbals

The *syrinx* or pan pipes.

The *auloi*, or double pipes. They were made of two separate pipes with a reed mouthpiece. The musician played the two pipes simultaneously.

The harp

The *timpanon*

Poetry

In Greece, music and poetry were closely linked. Poetry was usually performed in public, rather than read privately. The words were sung or chanted, often with a musical accompaniment.

Men called *rhapsodes* made their living by reciting poetry at religious festivals or at private parties. They knew long epic poems such as Homer's *Odyssey* and *Iliad* (see page 17) by heart.

This vase painting shows a *rhapsode* reciting from a podium.

Apollo and the Muses

Apollo was the god of music and poetry and is often shown with a lyre or a *kithara*. According to legend, the lyre was invented by Apollo's half-brother, Hermes, who gave the instrument to Apollo in exchange for some cattle which he had stolen from him.

Apollo is closely associated with nine goddesses called the Muses, who were believed to inspire and guide people's creative and intellectual activities. Each of them was responsible for a particular art, such as poetry, music or dance.

Parties and games

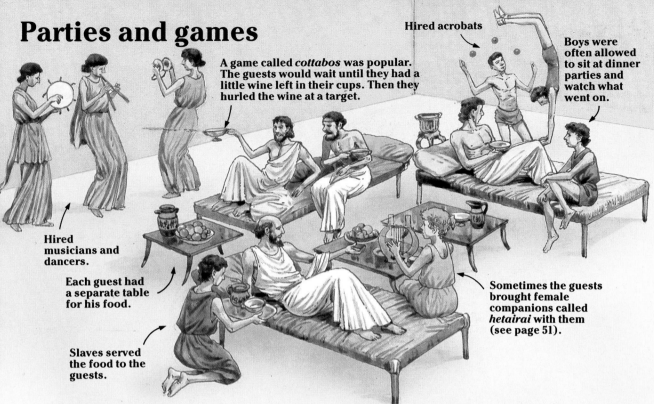

Hired acrobats

A game called *cottabos* was popular. The guests would wait until they had a little wine left in their cups. Then they hurled the wine at a target.

Boys were often allowed to sit at dinner parties and watch what went on.

Hired musicians and dancers.

Each guest had a separate table for his food.

Slaves served the food to the guests.

Sometimes the guests brought female companions called *hetairai* with them (see page 51).

Dinner parties were a favourite leisure activity. A man would invite several male friends to his house for a meal. The guests were met at the door by slaves who washed their hands and feet. Then they lay on couches in a room called the *andron*, where food was served by slaves. There was a choice of several dishes for each course.

Once the food was cleared away, the drinking and talking began. This was known as a *symposium*. The guests drank wine which had been mixed with water in a big vase called a *krater*. The conversation might be a serious discussion about some aspect of life, such as morals or politics. But often parties were more relaxed, with guests playing the lyre, reciting poetry, telling jokes or posing riddles. Additional entertainment might be provided by a troupe of hired musicians, dancers or acrobats.

Toys and games

Animal fighting was considered a sport. Cocks, quails, or a cat and dog would fight each other to the death.

This vase painting shows two warriors playing a board game similar to draughts or chess.

The Greeks also enjoyed sport. This carving shows a game which seems to resemble modern hockey.

Adults often played dice, either at home or in special gaming houses. Another favourite was a game called knuckle bones, in which small animal bones were thrown like dice.

Whipping top

Baby's rattle

Doll

Wealthy families gave their children many games and toys to amuse them

Hoop and stick

Yoyo

in their leisure hours. Some of them are shown here.

55

The theatre

The origins of theatre in the western world can be traced back to Ancient Greece. It developed from a countryside festival, held in honour of the god Dionysus. In Athens this developed into a more formal annual event, known as the *City Dionysia*. Songs were specially composed each year for the festival and were performed together with dances by a group of men known as a *chorus*. Prizes were awarded for the best entry.

At first, the *chorus* performed in the market place, but later a huge open-air theatre was built on the slopes of the Acropolis near the temple of Dionysus. Later, theatres were built all over the Greek world. Most of them could hold at least 18,000 spectators.

One of the best preserved Greek theatres is at Epidaurus. It was built on a hillside and could seat around 14,000 spectators.

The theatre building

The scene on the right is a reconstruction of a typical Greek theatre. It shows how it would have looked when a play was in progress.

Important people, such as leading citizens, distinguished foreign visitors or competition judges, sat at the front of the theatre. Special stone seats like this one were reserved for them.

The people from each district of a city had their own block of seats. Tokens like these were used as tickets. The letters on them show which block of benches the ticket-holder could sit in. Seats cost two obols. From the time of Pericles† the State paid for poor people's tickets.

The Athens theatre festival

In Athens the *Dionysia* was one of the city's most important religious celebrations. The festival, which lasted for five days, was a public holiday so that everyone could attend. The first day was devoted to processions and sacrifices. The remaining four days were taken up with drama competitions.

The *Dionysia* was organized by an official called an *archon* (see page 61). He picked a number of wealthy citizens, known as the *choregoi*, who had to pay for the production of the plays. Greek plays soon developed into two distinct types: tragedies and comedies. There were therefore two sections to the Athenian competition. Each year three tragic writers and five comedy writers were entered.

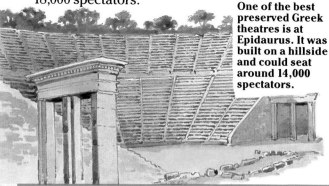

▲ Scene from a tragedy

▲ Scene from a comedy

▲ Scene from a *satyr* play

Tragedies were usually written about the heroes of the past. They concentrated on grand themes such as whether to obey or defy the will of the gods, human passions and conflicts, or the misuse of power. The best known tragic writers are Aeschylus†, Sophocles† and Euripides†.

In comedy, characters were usually ordinary people and the dialogue often included comments on the politics and personalities of the day. However, they also contained much clowning and slapstick humour and many rude jokes. The most famous comic writer is Aristophanes†.

In the comedy competition each author entered one play. However, a writer competing in the tragedy section had to enter three tragedies and a *satyr* play. This was a play which made fun of the tragic theme. The chorus were dressed as *satyrs* – wild followers of Dionysus who were half-man and half-beast.

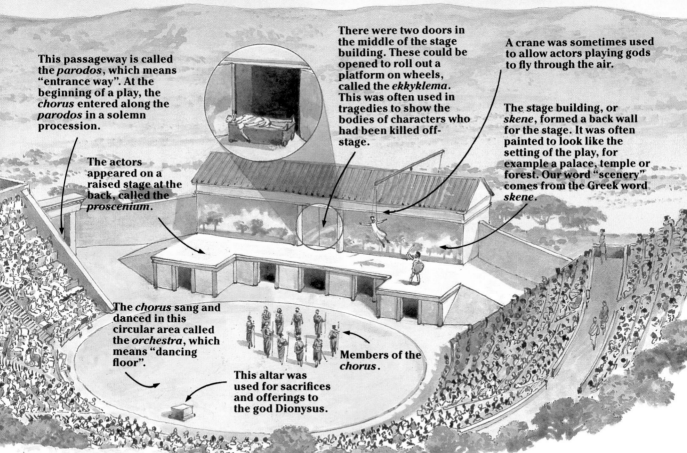

This passageway is called the *parodos*, which means "entrance way". At the beginning of a play, the *chorus* entered along the *parodos* in a solemn procession.

There were two doors in the middle of the stage building. These could be opened to roll out a platform on wheels, called the *ekkyklema*. This was often used in tragedies to show the bodies of characters who had been killed off-stage.

A crane was sometimes used to allow actors playing gods to fly through the air.

The stage building, or *skene*, formed a back wall for the stage. It was often painted to look like the setting of the play, for example a palace, temple or forest. Our word "scenery" comes from the Greek word *skene*.

The actors appeared on a raised stage at the back, called the *proscenium*.

The *chorus* sang and danced in this circular area called the *orchestra*, which means "dancing floor".

Members of the *chorus*.

This altar was used for sacrifices and offerings to the god Dionysus.

The performers

All the performers in Greek plays were men. At first, the play consisted simply of the *chorus* singing and dancing, but later an actor was introduced to exchange dialogue with the leader of the *chorus*. Thespis of Icarus is said to have been the first writer to use an actor in 530BC. Our word "thespian" comes from his name.

A second and third actor were later added, and they often played several roles each. The dialogue between the actors eventually became the most important part of the drama, with the *chorus* only commenting on the action.

Costumes

A *chorus* member dressed as a bird.

Male actor dressed as a woman.

Comic actors

Happy characters wore bright colours, and tragic ones dark colours. Because of the size of theatres, actors had to be visible and clothes were often padded to give them bulk. They wore large wigs and thick-soled shoes to look taller. In comedies, the *chorus* also wore costumes and sometimes even dressed as birds or animals.

Masks

Each actor wore a painted mask made of stiffened fabric or cork. The expression on the mask showed the character's age, sex and feelings. Actors could change parts quickly by simply swapping masks. The masks were easily visible, even from the back of the theatre. They had large, open mouths which amplified the actors' voices.

Athletics and sport

One of the most popular pastimes for Greek men was athletics. The Greek states encouraged their citizens to take part in sport because it kept them fit and meant that they would be in good fighting condition if there were a war.

There were many competitions which athletes could enter. Most were only local affairs, but four events (the Olympic, Pythian, Isthmian and Nemean Games) attracted competitors from all over the Greek world. They were known as the Panhellenic Games. Each one was held as part of a religious festival in honour of a particular deity.

The Olympic Games

The Olympic Games were the oldest and most important of the competitions. They probably developed from funeral games held in memory of the hero Pelops (see page 83). They started in 776BC and were held every four years at Olympia, in honour of Zeus. They lasted five days.

In the year of the Games, messengers travelled through Greece and the colonies, announcing the date of the Games and inviting people to attend.

All wars had to cease until the Games were over to allow people to travel to Olympia in safety.

At Olympia, a group of impressive buildings were built for the Games. These included sports grounds for the various events, facilities for the competitors and spectators, and temples for the religious ceremonies. This is a reconstruction of how Olympia would have looked at its height.

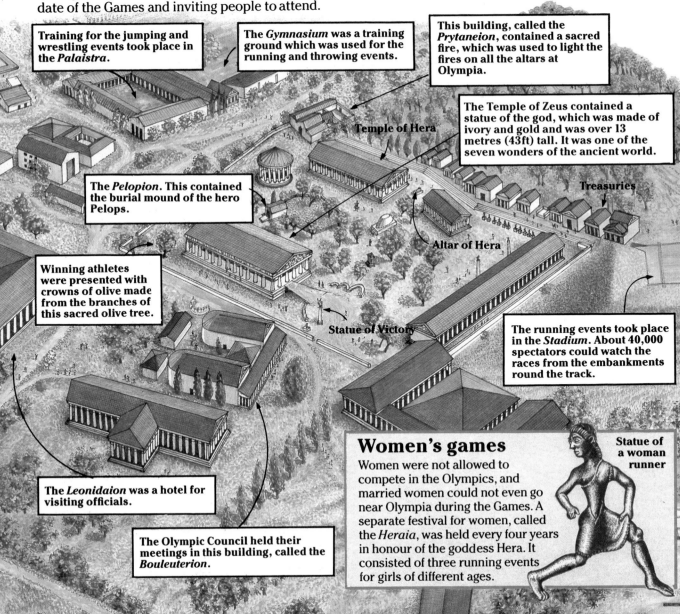

Training for the jumping and wrestling events took place in the *Palaistra*.

The *Gymnasium* was a training ground which was used for the running and throwing events.

This building, called the *Prytaneion*, contained a sacred fire, which was used to light the fires on all the altars at Olympia.

Temple of Hera

The Temple of Zeus contained a statue of the god, which was made of ivory and gold and was over 13 metres (43ft) tall. It was one of the seven wonders of the ancient world.

The *Pelopion*. This contained the burial mound of the hero Pelops.

Treasuries

Altar of Hera

Winning athletes were presented with crowns of olive made from the branches of this sacred olive tree.

Statue of Victory

The running events took place in the *Stadium*. About 40,000 spectators could watch the races from the embankments round the track.

The *Leonidaion* was a hotel for visiting officials.

The Olympic Council held their meetings in this building, called the *Bouleuterion*.

Women's games

Women were not allowed to compete in the Olympics, and married women could not even go near Olympia during the Games. A separate festival for women, called the *Heraia*, was held every four years in honour of the goddess Hera. It consisted of three running events for girls of different ages.

Statue of a woman runner

The events

Running

This vase painting shows a special race in which athletes wore a helmet and greaves† and carried a shield.

Running was the oldest event in the Games. The track in the Stadium was about 192 metres (640ft) long and was made of clay covered with sand. There were three main races: the *stade* (one length of the track), the *diaulos* (two lengths) and the *dolichos* (20 or 24 lengths).

Wrestling

There were three wrestling events. In upright wrestling, an athlete had to throw his opponent three times to win. In ground wrestling the contest went on until one man gave in. The third event, called the *pankration*, was even more dangerous, as any tactic except biting and eye-gouging was permitted.

The pentathlon

This vase painting shows a jumper, a discus thrower and two javelin throwers.

The *pentathlon* was a competition consisting of five athletic events: running, wrestling, jumping, discus and javelin throwing. It was designed to find the best all-round athlete. The *pentathlon* was a very demanding competition, which required great strength and endurance.

Boxing

At first, the contestants' hands were bound with leather thongs. Later, special boxing gloves were developed.

A boxing contest could go on for several hours and was only decided when one athlete lost consciousness or conceded defeat. Athletes therefore aimed most of their punches at their opponents' heads. Virtually any blow with the hand was permitted.

Chariot races

There were chariot races for teams of two or four horses. The course consisted of 12 laps round two posts in the ground. At the start, the chariots were released from a special starting gate. As many as 40 chariots could take part in one race, and collisions were common.

Horse races

The basic horse race was run over a distance of about 1200 metres. In another race the rider dismounted and ran the last stretch beside his horse. Jockeys rode bareback and accidents were common. The jockey was often employed by the horse's owner to race for him.

The winners

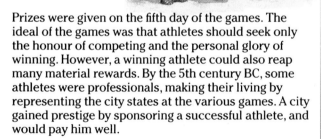

Winners were presented with an olive wreath, palm branches and woollen ribbons. They might also have a statue erected in their honour.

Prizes were given on the fifth day of the games. The ideal of the games was that athletes should seek only the honour of competing and the personal glory of winning. However, a winning athlete could also reap many material rewards. By the 5th century BC, some athletes were professionals, making their living by representing the city states at the various games. A city gained prestige by sponsoring a successful athlete, and would pay him well.

The modern Olympics

The ancient Olympics ended by AD395, when Olympia was destroyed by two violent earthquakes. In AD1896 a Frenchman called Baron Pierre de Coubertin was inspired by the ideals of the ancient competition and organized the first modern Olympic Games. Many aspects of the ancient games have been preserved. For example, some ancient games included a relay race in which a torch was passed from one runner to the next. The last runner of the winning team lit a fire on an altar. This event has been adapted for the modern Olympics as the lighting of the Olympic Flame.

59

Democracy in Athens

At the end of the Archaic Period, some Greek states overthrew their tyrants† (see page 21) and adopted a system of government called *democracy*. The name comes from the Greek words *demos* (people) and *kratos* (rule). Under this system all citizens (see page 20) had a say in the government of their city state.

These pages describe how democracy worked in Athens, because this is the state we know most about. Democracy was first introduced in Athens in 508BC by the leader Cleisthenes†. Today, the term democracy is used to describe a system in which everybody has a vote. However, in Ancient Greece only citizens had this right. All other social groups, such as women, foreign residents and slaves, were excluded.

Local organization

Cleisthenes split the people of Attica (Athens and the surrounding area) into different groups for administrative purposes.

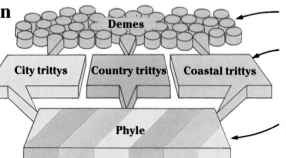

Attica was divided into many small communities called *demes*.

Demes were grouped into 30 larger groups called *trittyes*. Ten *trittyes* represented the city of Athens, ten the countryside and ten the coastal areas.

Trittyes were grouped into ten *phylai*, or tribes. Each *phyle* was made up of three *trittyes*: one *trittys* from the city, one from the country and one from the coast.

The Assembly

Every citizen had the right to speak and to vote at the Assembly, which met about once every ten days on a hill called the Pnyx. At least 6000 citizens had to be present for a meeting to take place. If too few people attended, special police were sent out to round up more citizens. The Assembly debated proposals which were put to it by the Council (see right). It could approve, change or reject the Council's suggestions.

An Assembly meeting on the Pnyx.

The Council

The 50 councillors on duty met in this building, called the Tholos. They kept it manned day and night, in case of emergency.

The Council drew up new laws and policies, which were then debated in the Assembly. The Council was made up of 500 citizens, 50 from each of the ten Athenian tribes. Councillors were chosen annually by lot. Each tribal group took it in turn to lead the Council, taking responsibility for the day-to-day running of the state.

The legal system

One of a citizen's duties was to participate in the running of the legal system. All citizens over 30 were expected to volunteer for jury service. From 461BC jurors were paid, to compensate them for any loss of earnings. There were no professional judges, lawyers or legal officials.

The Athenians tried to make their courts fair and unbiased. Each court had a jury of over 200 men, to ensure that jurors could not be bribed or intimidated.

As there were no lawyers, citizens had to conduct their own cases. Some people employed professional speech writers to prepare their cases for them. Only citizens could speak in court. If a *metic* was accused, he had to persuade a citizen to speak on his behalf.

Any citizen who wanted to serve as a juror simply went to the court. Often more people volunteered than were needed. This machine, called a *kleroteria*, was used to select the names of the jurors for that day.

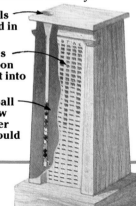

Coloured balls were dropped in here.

Jurors' names were written on cards and put into these slots.

The colour of ball next to each row decided whether those jurors would serve.

The archons

During the Archaic Period the *archons*† had been the most important officials (see page 21). Under democracy, much of their power passed to the *strategoi* (see below) and the *archons* retained only ceremonial duties. There were nine *archons*, chosen annually by lot from the citizens. Three of them were more important than the others and had special duties.

The *Basileus Archon* presided over the *Areopagus* (see page 21), arranged religious sacrifices, and organized the renting of temple land. He also supervised the theatre festival and other feasts.

The *Eponymous Archon* chose the men who were to finance the choral and drama contests (see page 56). He was also responsible for lawsuits about inheritances and the affairs of heiresses, orphans and widows.

The *Polemarch Archon* was in charge of offerings and special athletic contests held in honour of men killed in war. He also dealt with the legal affairs of *metics*† (foreign residents).

The strategoi

When Athens sent an army or navy into battle, it was led by one or two *strategoi*.

The *strategoi* were military commanders (see page 36) who also had the power to implement the policies decided by the Council and the Assembly. There were ten *strategoi*, one from each of the Athenian tribes. They were elected annually and could be re-elected many times. The *strategoi* had to answer to the Assembly for their actions and for the money they spent.

Ostracism

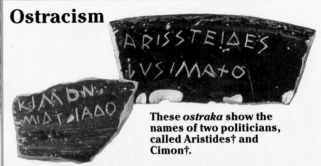

These *ostraka* show the names of two politicians, called Aristides† and Cimon†.

Ostracism was a system used to remove unpopular politicians. A vote of ostracism could be held once a year in the Assembly. Each citizen present wrote the name of any politician he wished to see banished on a piece of broken pottery, called an *ostrakon*. If more than 6000 votes were cast against a politician, he had to leave Athens for 10 years.

Each juror was issued with two different bronze tokens which were used for voting. At the end of the trial, he handed in one of them to show whether he thought the accused person was innocent or guilty.

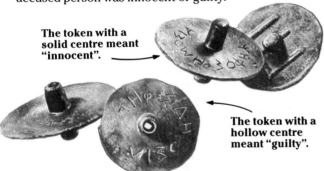

The token with a solid centre meant "innocent".

The token with a hollow centre meant "guilty".

Certain jurors, who were chosen by lot, were given special tasks. One took charge as the judge, four counted the votes and one worked a water clock like the one shown here. This was used to limit the time allowed to each speaker.

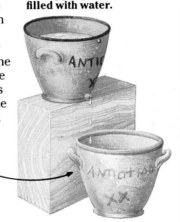

The upper pot was filled with water.

When all the water had run through into this lower pot, the speaker's time was up.

The Golden Age and the Peloponnesian War

The Persian Wars (see pages 40-41) were followed by an era of great achievement in Athens which is known as its Golden Age (479-431BC). Trade flourished and the city became very rich. Athens became a great centre for the arts, attracting the best sculptors, potters, architects, dramatists, historians and philosophers. This security was shattered by the outbreak of the Peloponnesian War between Athens and Sparta. It lasted for 27 years (431-404BC) and tore the Greek world apart. The city states were left weak and exhausted, and Athens never regained her former power.

During the Golden Age, the city was improved and the temples on the Acropolis† were rebuilt.

Pericles

The democratic system (see pages 60-61) was finalized during this period. The most famous politician was Pericles†, who dominated Athenian politics from 443-429BC. He was a very powerful public speaker and could usually persuade the Assembly to vote the way he wanted. He was so popular that he was elected *strategos* year after year. One of his most important achievements was to organize the rebuilding of the Acropolis.

Bust of Pericles

Relations between Sparta and Athens

Soon after the end of the Persian Wars, relations between Sparta and Athens started to deteriorate. As Athens became more powerful and wealthy, the Spartans felt threatened.

In c.460BC the *helots* and the Messenians (see page 22) rebelled against the Spartans. The Spartans asked the Athenians for help, but by the time the Athenians arrived, the Spartans had changed their minds. They were so distrustful of democrats that they would not let the Athenians intervene and instead sent them home. The Athenians felt bitterly insulted and abandoned their alliance with Sparta.

The Long Walls

In 460BC the Athenians began building enormous walls linking their city to its port at Piraeus. They are known as the Long Walls. They prevented an enemy cutting Athens off from her navy and made the city into an enormous fortress. The Spartans thought this meant that Athens was preparing for war, and fighting broke out between the two states in 448-447BC. After this, Sparta and Athens signed a treaty known as the Thirty Years' Peace, but relations between them remained hostile.

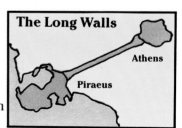

The Long Walls

Athens

Piraeus

The start of the Peloponnesian War

In 431BC hostilities broke out between Corinth and its colony of Corcyra (modern Corfu). Sparta supported Corinth and Athens backed Corcyra. This began the Peloponnesian War, so called because Sparta was supported by a league of states in the Peloponnese (the southern part of mainland Greece). Athens was backed by its allies in the Delian League (see page 41).

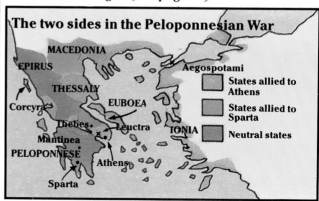

The two sides in the Peloponnesian War

MACEDONIA
EPIRUS
Aegospotami
THESSALY
Corcyra
EUBOEA
Thebes
Leuctra
IONIA
Mantinea
PELOPONNESE
Athens
Sparta

States allied to Athens

States allied to Sparta

Neutral states

The Spartans had a very powerful army and were nearly unbeatable in land battles. They were easily able to invade Attica†. The Athenians had a superior navy and a weaker army than the Spartans. They therefore tried to avoid fighting the Spartans on land. Instead, they stayed inside their city walls and were able to import food by sea. This resulted in a long deadlock.

The Spartan army devastated the countryside around Athens, but could not get through the Long Walls.

The Sicilian expedition

In 430BC a plague broke out in Athens. It lasted four years and about a quarter of the population died, including Pericles. By 421BC both sides were exhausted and signed a peace treaty.

However, war broke out again and events soon turned against Athens. In 415BC a politician called Alcibiades† persuaded the Athenians to send an expedition against the city of Syracuse on Sicily. Before the attack began, Alcibiades was told to return to Athens to face charges brought against him by his enemies. Instead, he fled to Sparta and advised the Spartans how to defeat Athens. The Athenians were defeated at Syracuse and many of their troops were massacred.

About 7000 of the surviving Athenians were forced to work in stone quarries on Sicily, where many of them died.

Political unrest in Athens

After this catastrophe, life in Athens became very unsettled. In 411BC a council of 400 men seized power and abolished democracy†. The news caused the Athenian forces overseas to mutiny. After three months, democracy was restored. The Athenians badly needed a strong leader, so they decided to recall Alcibiades and appoint him *strategos*, despite his earlier treachery. But he failed to fulfil their hopes and was not re-elected. Support for the Athenians declined and several of their allies withdrew from the Delian League.

The Spartans build a fleet

Meanwhile the Persians intervened. They were fighting the Greek colonists in Ionia, who were supported by the Spartans. The Persians persuaded the Spartans to withdraw from Ionia by giving them money to build a fleet. This enabled the Spartans to attack the Athenians at sea as well as on land.

The Battle of Aegospotami

In 405BC the Spartans scored a decisive naval victory. They launched a surprise attack on the Athenian fleet when it was in harbour at a place called Aegospotami in Thrace. The Spartans captured 170 Athenian ships and executed about 4000 prisoners. It was a blow from which Athens never recovered.

The Athenians had gone ashore at Aegospotami to eat when the Spartans attacked.

The Spartans then laid siege to Athens. Without a fleet to support them, the Athenians were unable to import food, and many people starved. In 404BC they had to surrender. The Spartans insisted that the Long Walls were pulled down, ended the Delian League and abolished democracy. They installed an oligarchic† government known as the Thirty Tyrants.

After the Peloponnesian War

The Spartans' victory did not bring peace or unity to Greece. They began to lose control in Athens, where democracy was restored in 403BC despite their disapproval. Wars broke out again between the various states. Most Greeks were too absorbed in these problems to notice a new power rising in Macedonia, to the north-east. The Macedonians began expanding their territory, and took advantage of the lack of unity in Greece. Within 50 years of the end of the Peloponnesian War, the Macedonians had conquered many of the Greek states (see page 72).

Key dates

479-431BC The Golden Age of Athens.

460BC The Spartans reject Athenian help in stopping a rebellion. The Athenians start to build the Long Walls.

431BC Start of the Peloponnesian War.

415-413BC Athens sends an expedition to Sicily which is defeated.

405BC The Spartans defeat the Athenian fleet at the Battle of Aegospotami.

404BC The Athenians surrender. End of the Peloponnesian War.

371BC The Spartans are defeated by the Thebans at the Battle of Leuctra and Thebes becomes a leading power in Greece.

362BC The Thebans are defeated by the Spartans and Athenians at the Battle of Mantinea.

Gods and goddesses

The Greeks believed in the existence of many divine beings, who looked after all aspects of life and death. They thought of the gods as being in many ways like humans – they got married, had children and showed human characteristics such as love, jealousy or deceitfulness. Many legends were told to describe the gods' personalities and teach what pleased or angered them.

How the world began

According to legend, Gaea (Mother Earth) rose out of chaos. She gave birth to a son, Uranos (Sky), who became her husband. They had many children, the most important of whom were the fourteen Titans. One of them, Cronos, led the others in a rebellion against their father and deposed him.

Cronos married his sister, Rhea. Their youngest son, Zeus, led his brothers and sisters against the Titans. He deposed Cronos and became the leader of the new gods. The new rulers lived on Mount Olympus and were known as the Olympians.

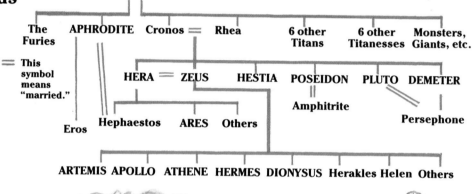

The battle between the Titans and the Olympians

The Olympian gods

This family tree shows some of the Greek deities. The most important and powerful of them were the 12 Olympians, whose names are written in capitals. Some of the legends associated with them are told below. Most of the gods had their own special symbols.

Uranos = Gaea

The Furies — APHRODITE — Cronos = Rhea — 6 other Titans — 6 other Titanesses — Monsters, Giants, etc.

= This symbol means "married."

HERA = ZEUS — HESTIA — POSEIDON — PLUTO — DEMETER

Amphitrite

Eros — Hephaestos — ARES — Others

Persephone

ARTEMIS APOLLO ATHENE HERMES DIONYSUS Herakles Helen Others

Zeus

Zeus was the ruler of the gods and controlled the heavens. He was married to his sister Hera, but was frequently unfaithful to her. He had many affairs with mortal women and appeared to them in various disguises, such as a bull, a shower of gold or a swan.

Zeus' symbols: the thunderbolt, eagle and oak tree.

Hera

Hera was the sister and wife of Zeus. She was the protector of women and of marriage. She was beautiful and proud, and bitterly resented her husband's affairs with other women. She often persecuted his lovers and their children.

Hera's symbols: the pomegranate and the peacock.

Poseidon

Poseidon was the brother of Zeus and the ruler of the seas. His home was an underwater palace, where he kept his gold chariot and white horses. Poseidon was also known as the earth-shaker, because he was thought to cause earthquakes.

Poseidon's symbols: the trident, dolphins and horses.

Hestia

Hestia was the goddess of the hearth. Every Greek city and family had a shrine dedicated to her. She was gentle and pure, and stood aloof from the constant quarrels of the other gods. Eventually she resigned her throne on Olympus, knowing that she would receive a welcome wherever she went.

Pluto

Pluto drove a gold chariot with black horses.

◀ Pluto ruled the Underworld, the Kingdom of the Dead. He guarded the dead jealously, rarely letting any of them return to Earth. He owned all the precious metals and gems of the Earth. Pluto kidnapped and married his niece, Persephone.*

Demeter

◀ Demeter was the godd[...] plants. When her daug[...] Persephone was kidna[...] Demeter neglected the plants and went to search for her. This caused winter. When Persephone returned to her mother, she brought the spring and summer.*

Demeter's symbol: a sheaf of wheat or barley.

Aphrodite

Aphrodite was the goddess of love and beauty. She was born in the sea and rode to shore on a scallop shell. Aphrodite was married to Hephaestos, but loved Ares. She charmed everyone, as she wore a golden belt which made her irresistibly attractive.

Aphrodite's symbols: roses, doves, sparrows, dolphins and rams.

Hephaestos

Hephaestos was a smith whose ▶ forge was beneath Mount Etna in Sicily. He built Zeus' golden throne and his shield, which caused storms and thunder when it was shaken. He was the patron of craftsmen and the long-suffering husband of Aphrodite.

Ares

Ares' symbols: a burning torch, spear, dogs and vultures.

◀ Ares was the god of war and Aphrodite's lover. He was short tempered and violent. He once had to stand trial for murder in Athens on the hill of the Areopagus (see page 43), which was named after him.

Artemis

◀ Artemis was the moon goddess. Her silver arrows brought plague and death, though she could heal as well. She protected young girls and pregnant women. Artemis was the mistress of all wild animals and enjoyed hunting in her chariot pulled by stags.

Artemis' symbols: cypress trees, deer and dogs.

Apollo

Apollo was the twin brother of ▶ Artemis. He was the god of the sun, light and truth. Music, poetry, science and healing were also under his control. Apollo killed his mother's enemy, the serpent Python, when it was sheltering in the shrine at Delphi. He seized the shrine and made Delphi his Oracle (see page 68).

Apollo's symbol: the laurel tree.

Hermes

Hermes was a precocious and ▶ naughty child, full of tricks and cunning, who stole cattle from Apollo and invented the lyre†. He became the messenger of the gods and was also the patron of travellers and thieves. He was said to have invented the alphabet, mathematics, astronomy and boxing.

Hermes wore a winged hat and sandals and carried a staff.

Athene

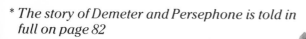

Athene's symbols: the owl and the olive tree.

◀ Athene was the daughter of Zeus and Metis the Titaness. Zeus swallowed Metis because of a prophecy that if she had a son he would depose his father. One day Zeus had a headache and ordered Hephaestos to crack his skull open. Athene sprang out, fully armed. She was the goddess of wisdom and war and the patron deity of Athens.

Dioynsus

◀ Dionysus was god of the vine, wine and fertility. He wandered the world teaching people how to make wine, accompanied by wild and fanatical followers. When Hestia resigned her place on Olympus, Dionysus became one of the 12 Olympians.

Dionysus carried a special staff, called a thyrsus.

* *The story of Demeter and Persephone is told in full on page 82*

65

emples, worship and festivals

As the Greeks thought of their gods as having the same needs as human beings, they believed that the gods needed somewhere to live on Earth.

Temples were built as the gods' earthly homes. The basic design of temples developed from the royal halls of the Mycenaean Age (see page 13).

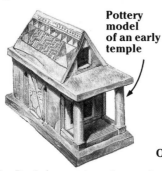

Pottery model of an early temple

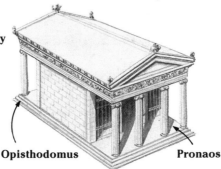

Opisthodomus **Pronaos**

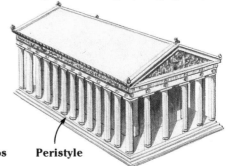

Peristyle

In the Dark Ages, a temple consisted of a room, called a *cella*, with a pillared porch in front. The *cella* contained a special statue of the god, known as the cult statue.

This more elaborate style of temple developed in the early Archaic Period. It had a porch at the front, called the *pronaos*, and another at the back, the *opisthodomus*.

This later Archaic temple was built on a platform and had several steps leading up to the entrance. There was a covered row of columns, called a *peristyle*, round the outside.

The Parthenon

In the Classical Period temples became much larger and more elaborate. This reconstruction shows the Parthenon in Athens, which was built in 447-438BC.

The exterior was decorated with friezes and statues showing mythological scenes, which were painted in bright colours.

A second room behind the *cella* was used as a treasury. Offerings such as jewellery, vases and statues were stored here.

The cult statue of the goddess Athene was made of gold and ivory and was over 12 metres (40ft) high. Athene held a figure of Nike, the goddess of victory, in one hand and a spear and shield in the other.

Cella

The building was made of marble.

A *peristyle* surrounded the whole structure.

The altar

There was a stone altar outside a temple, often situated in front of the main entrance. People brought animals or birds as offerings to the temple deity and they were sacrificed by a priest at the altar.

Festivals

The Greeks held many religious festivals in honour of their gods. The purpose of a festival was to please the gods and persuade them to grant the people's wishes. This could be by making the crops grow or bringing victory in war. Festivals did not consist solely of religious ceremonies – other events, such as athletic competitions or theatrical performances, could also be held. These events included things which would especially please the particular god. For example, at the Pythian Games, which were dedicated to Apollo, victors were presented with crowns of laurel, which was Apollo's sacred plant.

The dress for the goddess Athene was displayed on the mast of a ship, which was dragged along in the procession.

Priests and priestesses

Soldiers

Important citizens

Musicians and dancers

Offering bearers

Sacrificial beasts

The period of the festival was a public holiday so that the whole population of Athens could watch the procession.

The Great Panathenaea

The most important festival in Athens was the *Great Panathenaea*, the feast of the goddess Athene. It was held every four years, and lasted for six days. It included music, poetry recitals and sports events. The climax of the festival was a huge procession from the Dipylon Gate to the Erechtheum temple on the Acropolis†. There a specially made dress was offered to an ancient wooden statue of Athene, which was said to have fallen from heaven in ancient times.

The Anthesteria

A spring festival, called the *Anthesteria*, was held in Athens each February. The wine from the last harvest was put on sale and a statue of Dionysus, the god of wine, was carried in triumph to his temple. On the final day of the festival, each family prepared a meal for the spirits of the dead and left it on the altar in their house.

During the *Anthesteria*, children were given special jugs (see page 52).

Worship

Private worship played an important part in Greek religion. A family would say prayers every day at the altar in the courtyard of their house. During prayers an offering of wine, called a *libation*, was poured over the altar. People would also pray to the appropriate gods as they went about their daily life. For example, someone going on a journey would pray to Hermes, the god of travellers.

If someone wanted to ask the gods for a particular favour, they would go to the temple of the appropriate deity and make a sacrifice. This could be cakes, a libation, a bird or an animal.

There were rules on how to please the various gods. For example, different species of birds and animals were acceptable to different gods. If the rules were not followed, the offering might not be acceptable. Each god had his or her own priests, who ensured that sacrifices were made correctly.

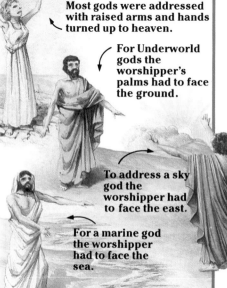
Most gods were addressed with raised arms and hands turned up to heaven.

For Underworld gods the worshipper's palms had to face the ground.

To address a sky god the worshipper had to face the east.

For a marine god the worshipper had to face the sea.

Oracles and mystery cults

The Greeks never began an important project without first trying to learn the will of the gods. Often they would visit an oracle, where a special priest or priestess could speak on behalf of a god.

Other popular ways of learning what the future might hold were reading omens or consulting a soothsayer (someone who could foresee the future).

Oracles

There were several oracles* in Greece where people could ask the gods questions about personal or national problems. The most famous one was at Delphi, where the god Apollo was believed to speak through his priestess, the Pythia. At first the Pythia gave oracles once a year, but Delphi became so popular that they were given every week and two priestesses were needed. Many Greek states regularly sent deputations to Delphi for advice on political affairs.

The temple priests put people's questions to the Pythia. They then interpreted her replies. These were often vague and could be interpreted in more than one way.

The Pythia gave her oracles in an inner sanctuary. First she bathed in a holy fountain, drank water from a sacred spring and inhaled the smoke of burning laurel leaves. This reconstruction shows what a consultation might have looked like.

The Pythia dressed in white and sat on a tripod. She held a branch of laurel in her hand.

The inner sanctuary was closed off from the priests by a curtain.

She gave her oracles in a trance, which was said to be caused by fumes rising from a cleft in the rocks.

Omens

Interpreting omens was a skilled art, and was only undertaken by specially trained priests. Omens could be read from many different things, such as blemishes on the livers of sacrificed animals, the flight of birds or thunder and lightning.

Soothsayers

◀ The Greeks believed that certain people, called soothsayers or seers, could foresee the future. According to legend, Cassandra, a princess of Troy, had these powers. When she broke a promise to the god Apollo, he decreed that no-one would ever believe her prophecies. Cassandra warned the people of Troy that the wooden horse was a trick, but they ignored her and so the city was destroyed.

Fate and fortune

The Greeks believed that each person's destiny was decided by three goddesses called the Fates. Clotho spun the thread of life. Lachesis wound the thread and allotted a person's destiny. Atropos cut the thread, causing a person to die.

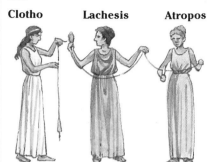

Clotho   Lachesis   Atropos

The goddess of fortune was called Tyche. She could shower people with gifts from her horn of plenty, but she also juggled with a ball, showing how someone could be up one day and down the next.

The word oracle can mean the priestess who spoke for the god, the sacred place where she could be consulted, or the message she gave.

Mystery cults

Many Greeks who were looking for a deeper religious faith joined one of the mystery cults. These were secret groups of worshippers associated with particular deities. The cults promised their members an answer to the meaning of life and a happy life after death. People who undertook the necessary training and led virtuous lives were initiated (introduced) by stages into the cult.

The most famous and popular was the cult of the goddesses Demeter and Persephone at Eleusis. The cult's main initiation ceremony, called the Greater Mysteries, was held in September. The mysteries continued to be celebrated at Eleusis until AD394.

The procession

The Greater Mysteries started with several days of sacrifices and purification. On the fifth day, a great procession set out from Athens to travel to Eleusis. They arrived at night, by torchlight.

Priestesses carried the sacred objects of the cult in baskets on their heads.

Statue of the goddess

The initiates wore white robes

The initiation ceremony

No-one knows exactly what happened at an initiation ceremony because it took place in private and the initiates were sworn to secrecy. This reconstruction shows what may have happened during an initiation.

This priestess, holding a pomegranate, played Persephone.

There may have been an enactment of the deeds of the goddesses. This priestess played the part of Demeter.

People waiting to be initiated.

People who had reached the higher stages of initiation were known as "viewers". They were probably shown something special, such as the sacred cult objects.

The origin of the Eleusinian mysteries

The cult of Demeter and Persephone was founded by Prince Triptolemus of Eleusis. According to legend*, when Persephone was kidnapped Demeter wandered the Earth searching for her, disguised as a poor old woman. When she arrived at Eleusis, the royal family took her in and gave her a job, caring for the royal children.

After Persephone was returned to Demeter, the two goddesses went back to Eleusis. They gave the king's son, Prince Triptolemus, a bag of grain and showed him how to plant and reap. Triptolemus travelled all over Greece teaching people how to grow grain and then returned to Eleusis, where he built a temple and established the cult of Demeter and Persephone.

This carving shows Prince Triptolemus with the two goddesses.

You can read the full story of Demeter and Persephone on page 82.

...and the Underworld

...s believed that when people died, their
...t to the Underworld. This was an
...und kingdom, sometimes known as
Hades, which was ruled by the god Pluto. The
picture below is an imaginative reconstruction of
what the Greeks thought would happen to them
when they arrived in the world of the dead.

Many caves and fissures on Earth were thought to be entrances to the Underworld. The soul was guided by the god Hermes through one of these entrances to the banks of the River Styx. The river marked the boundary between the world of the living and the Underworld. ▼

On the other side of the river, the soul passed the three-headed dog Cerberus. His job was to stop living intruders entering the Underworld and to prevent any of Pluto's subjects from escaping. ▲

Next the soul arrived at a cross-roads where Minos, Rhadamanthys and Aeacus judged all the newly-arrived souls. Their judgement was based on how the person had behaved in his or her earthly life. ▲

Souls whose relatives had provided them with a coin (see below) paid Charon the ferryman to take them across the river. Souls without the fare wandered lost and comfortless on the bank. ▲

Funerals

The purpose of Greek funeral rites was to ensure that the dead person's soul arrived safely in the Underworld. Ordinary Greeks were terrified by the thought that they might not receive a funeral. Without proper rituals, they believed that the soul would wander sadly by the River Styx and would not be able to enter the Underworld.

Visitors washed when they left, as death was thought to be unclean.

When someone died, their relatives and friends wore black and women cut their hair short as signs of mourning. The dead body lay in state at home for a day, so that people could come to pay their respects. The body was carefully dressed and arranged. A coin was placed in its mouth to enable the soul to pay the fare to cross the River Styx.

Even after the funeral, the continued well-being of the dead depended to some extent on the care of the living. Families made offerings to their ancestors on the anniversaries of their births and deaths, and at special festivals for the dead.

A wealthy family hired musicians and professional mourners to join the procession.

Early on the morning of the funeral a procession formed at the dead person's house. The body was either placed on a cart or on a bier carried by the relatives and friends. The body was then taken to the cemetery. The procession was a noisy affair, as it was the custom to express grief publicly with tears, sobbing and wailing.

Souls of initiates could ask to be born again. If they got to the Elysian Fields three times by leading virtuous or initiated lives, they could then go to the Isles of the Blessed. This was a place of eternal joy, ruled by Cronos, the leader of the Titans.

People who had led virtuous lives, along with initiates of the mystery cults †, were sent to the Elysian Fields, a happy place filled with golden sunlight.

The Pool of Memory

The souls of people who had led wicked or cruel existences on Earth were sent to Tartarus, where they were condemned to eternal punishment.

Another road led to Erebus, the palace of Pluto and Persephone. By the palace were two pools.

Initiates of the mystery cults chose the Pool of Memory which was shaded by white poplars. This enabled them to remember the secrets of the cult and pass straight to the Elysian Fields.

The Palace of Pluto and Persephone.

Most people had not been very good or very bad in their earthly life and so were sent to the Asphodel Fields. This was a grey, boring place where the souls drifted around aimlessly in the shade, waiting for offerings from the land of the living to cheer them up.

The Pool of Lethe (forgetfulness) was shaded by cypresses and ordinary souls drank there.

Tombs

Cemeteries were usually situated outside the city walls. Each family had its own burial plot, where members of the family were either buried or cremated. It was customary to bury personal belongings, such as jewellery, clothes or armour, with the dead person. Food, drink and bronze or pottery vessels were also buried for the soul to use in the afterlife.

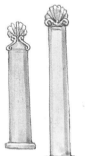

◄ Early tombs were marked by a plain marble slab, topped with a sculptured decoration.

A rich person would be buried in a stone coffin called a *sarcophagus*. This often had elaborately carved reliefs on the sides.

Sarcophagus

Stele

◄ By the 5th century BC, people who could afford it built elaborate tombs which looked like small temples. These were often decorated with portraits of the dead person carved on stone slabs, called *stelae*.

Lekythoi

The women of the family continued ► to bring offerings to the tomb long after the funeral. Perfume was often offered to the dead. It was carried in special white pottery vases called *lekythoi*. They were nearly solid, with only a tiny space for the perfume.

The rise of Macedonia

Macedonia lies in the north east of Greece (see map below). The Macedonian people claimed to be descendants of Macedon, son of Zeus. Although they thought of themselves as Greek, many Greeks considered Macedonia to be a cultural and political backwater, whose inhabitants were little better than barbarians†. Although the Macedonians spoke Greek, they had such a strong accent that it was said to be impossible to understand them.

During the 6th and 5th centuries BC, Macedonia was invaded many times. In 399BC the king was murdered and the country entered 40 years of instability and civil war (see date box below).

This ended with the accession of Philip II in 359BC. When he came to the throne, Macedonia had lost a lot of its territory and was split by political rivalries. Many of its soldiers had been killed and the country was impoverished.

Small ivory head of Philip, found in his tomb.

However, within 25 years Philip had united the country, extended the frontiers and turned Macedonia into the greatest military power of the day. He was a brilliant soldier and organizer, a fine speaker and a cunning diplomat with great personal charm. Even so, critics, such as the Athenian politician Demosthenes, saw him as a threat to democracy and independence.

The woman shown on this gold medallion is Philip's wife, Olympias.

The Macedonian royal family

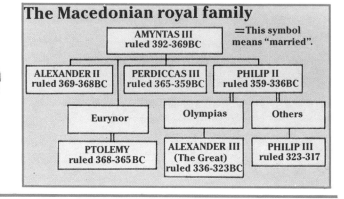

AMYNTAS III
ruled 392-369BC

= This symbol means "married".

ALEXANDER II ruled 369-368BC	PERDICCAS III ruled 365-359BC	PHILIP II ruled 359-336BC

Eurynor	Olympias	Others

PTOLEMY ruled 368-365BC	ALEXANDER III (The Great) ruled 336-323BC	PHILIP III ruled 323-317

Philip's conquests

Philip quickly brought Macedonia under control. In 357BC he started to expand his territory, first east and then south. By 342BC Philip controlled the whole of Thrace, Chalkidike and Thessaly (see map).

In 342BC the remaining Greek states, led by Athens and Thebes, formed the Hellenic League against him. Philip defeated them in 338BC at the battle of Chaeronea and gained control of Greece. He joined all the Greek states together in the League of Corinth, of which he was the *hegemon*, or leader. In 337BC he united Greece and Macedonia in a common cause by announcing a war against Persia.

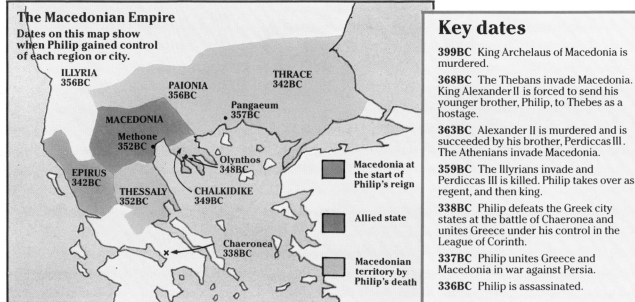

The Macedonian Empire

Dates on this map show when Philip gained control of each region or city.

ILLYRIA
356BC

PAIONIA
356BC

THRACE
342BC

Pangaeum
• 357BC

MACEDONIA

Methone
352BC •

Olynthos
348BC

EPIRUS
342BC

THESSALY
352BC

CHALKIDIKE
349BC

Chaeronea
338BC

Macedonia at the start of Philip's reign

Allied state

Macedonian territory by Philip's death

Key dates

399BC King Archelaus of Macedonia is murdered.

368BC The Thebans invade Macedonia. King Alexander II is forced to send his younger brother, Philip, to Thebes as a hostage.

363BC Alexander II is murdered and is succeeded by his brother, Perdiccas III. The Athenians invade Macedonia.

359BC The Illyrians invade and Perdiccas III is killed. Philip takes over as regent, and then king.

338BC Philip defeats the Greek city states at the battle of Chaeronea and unites Greece under his control in the League of Corinth.

337BC Philip unites Greece and Macedonia in war against Persia.

336BC Philip is assassinated.

The army

At the beginning of his reign, Philip reorganized the army and began a programme of intensive training. This produced a tough, well-disciplined army which was the most effective fighting force of the day. Philip led his troops in person, showing great bravery.

Soldiers at the back held their spears upright.

Soldiers in the first ranks held their spears out in front of them.

Each soldier wore a helmet, cuirass† and a bronze shield. He was armed with a short sword and a long spear called a *sarissa*.

The Macedonian infantry originally consisted of lightly-armed *peltasts* (see page 37). Philip gave them heavier armour and long spears and taught them to fight in a phalanx, shown above. They attacked by charging into the enemy's lines with their spears extended. This was a very effective tactic and proved to be a decisive factor in Philip's military successes.

There were elite units called the Companion Infantry and the Companion Cavalry. The sons of Macedonian noblemen were often educated at court and served as royal pages before joining the Companion Cavalry. This mosaic shows two royal pages out hunting.

Philip made great use of the Companion Cavalry, which he developed from the king's mounted bodyguard. They wore cuirasses, helmets and boots and were armed with long spears and swords.

Philip's death

Philip had several wives, but only one queen, Olympias. Her son, Alexander, was accepted as Philip's heir. In 337BC Philip took another wife, Cleopatra, and set Olympias aside. He was assassinated soon after. The assassin could have been a political opponent, but it is also possible that Olympias or Alexander had paid him.

In AD1977 archaeologists discovered a new tomb in the royal graveyard at Vergina. In the inner chamber they found a casket, containing the cremated remains of a man aged 40-50. Experts have since been able to piece together the skull.

It had a hole near the right eye. This proves that it was almost certainly Philip, who had been hit in the face by an arrow and lost his right eye.

Philip's tomb was buried under a mound of earth which protected it from grave robbers. This cutaway reconstruction shows the tomb and some of the treasures that were found in it.

This chamber contained the remains of a second body, probably Philip's wife Cleopatra.

Philip's burial chamber

This gold casket held Philip's ashes. The star symbol was the emblem of the Macedonian royal family.

Cuirass

Several pieces of Philip's armour were buried with him.

Helmet

Main entrance

Alexander the Great

Alexander became King of Macedonia in 336BC after the murder of his father, Philip (see page 73). He was only 20. He immediately embarked on a career of military conquests, which gained him the largest empire the Ancient World had known and earned him the title of Alexander the Great. He was a military genius, who inspired great loyalty in his followers and who had extraordinary energy and courage.

In 334BC Alexander led 35,000 troops into Asia Minor to attack the Persians (see page 41). This began an 11-year campaign, during which he captured vast territories in Asia Minor, Egypt, Afghanistan, Iran and India.

This reconstruction shows the Battle of Issus (333BC), at which Alexander defeated the Persians. It is based on a Roman mosaic in Pompeii.

Picture of Alexander taken from a Roman mosaic.

During his travels, Alexander founded many new cities, most of which he named "Alexandria", after himself. The most famous of these was the port of Alexandria in Egypt, which became the country's new capital.

Alexander did little to change the administration of the lands he seized, although he usually replaced the local governors with his own men. He left Greeks behind in all the areas he conquered, which helped to spread Greek language and culture across an enormous area. This Greek influence lasted long after Alexander's empire had collapsed.

Alexander realized that his empire was too big to be administered from Greece. In Persia, he tried to include Persians in the government to help unify the empire. He planned to give them equal rights and to let them serve in the army. The whole empire was to have one currency, and use Greek as the official language. Alexander himself adopted Persian dress and married a Persian noblewoman called Roxane.

In 323BC, Alexander died of a fever. He does not seem to have made plans for the government of the empire after his death. Although Roxane was pregnant with Alexander's heir, his generals soon divided the empire up between themselves (see pages 76-77).

Alexander was often shown on coins of the time.

Map of Alexander's empire

This map shows Alexander's route and the extent of the empire he conquered. The dates show when Alexander gained control of each region.

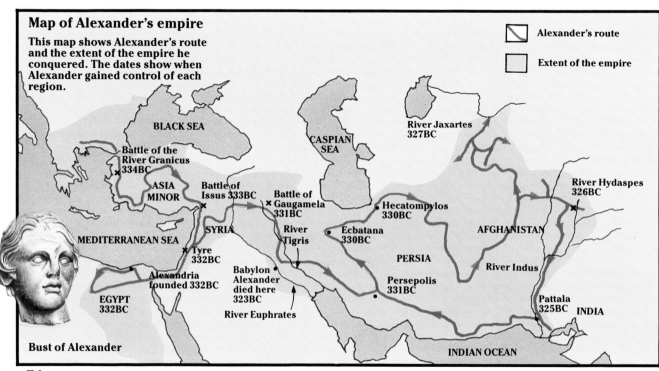

Alexander's route

Extent of the empire

BLACK SEA

CASPIAN SEA

River Jaxartes 327BC

Battle of the River Granicus 334BC

ASIA MINOR

Battle of Issus 333BC

Battle of Gaugamela 331BC

Hecatompylos 330BC

River Hydaspes 326BC

SYRIA

River Tigris

Ecbatana 330BC

AFGHANISTAN

MEDITERRANEAN SEA

Tyre 332BC

PERSIA

River Indus

Alexandria founded 332BC

Babylon Alexander died here 323BC

Persepolis 331BC

Pattala 325BC

EGYPT 332BC

River Euphrates

INDIA

Bust of Alexander

INDIAN OCEAN

Alexander's army

Alexander inherited a large, well-trained army with high morale. He invaded Persia with an army of 30,000 infantry and 5000 cavalry. Macedonian troops, known as the Royal Army, formed the core of the army. It also contained troops supplied by conquered provinces, such as Thessaly and the states of the Corinthian League, along with professional hired soldiers from all over Greece.

The cavalry

The basic cavalry unit consisted of 49 men. It charged in a wedge-shaped formation with the commander at the front. The cavalry was normally used to break up a phalanx† of enemy foot soldiers.

The cavalry often attacked by charging at the right end of the phalanx, which was its weakest point (see page 37). A phalanx of foot soldiers could then move in from behind to finish off the enemy in hand-to-hand fighting.

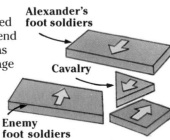

Alexander's foot soldiers

Cavalry

Enemy foot soldiers

The bulk of the cavalry was made up of horsemen from Thessaly, along with troops from the states of the Corinthian League. The elite troops, known as the Companion Cavalry, consisted of eight squadrons, made up of Macedonian noblemen.

Cavalryman from Thessaly

Member of the Companion Cavalry

The infantry

Like the cavalry, the infantry was made up of many different groups – foot soldiers, javelin men, archers and slingers. Alexander continued to use the elite Companion Infantry (see page 73), and he also had a royal bodyguard known as the *hypaspists*.

Foot soldiers continued to fight in a phalanx. Alexander often used the phalanx in an oblique formation, shown here. It enabled him to attack the weaker right wing of an enemy phalanx.

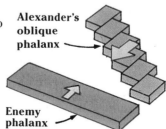

Alexander's oblique phalanx

Enemy phalanx

Under Alexander, many infantry soldiers went back to using the heavy bronze armour of the Greek *hoplites*†, although they still carried the Macedonian *sarissa* (spear). This picture shows a member of the Companion Infantry.

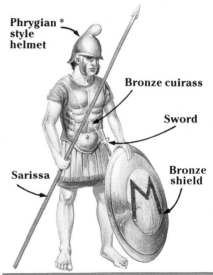

Phrygian * style helmet

Bronze cuirass

Sword

Sarissa

Bronze shield

The army on the move

Each soldier was expected to carry his own weapons and armour, as well as a personal pack containing bedding and cooking equipment. Pack animals and baggage wagons were used to carry bulky equipment such as tents, waterskins and siege equipment, and to move wounded men. The army was accompanied by servants and grooms, and by many women and children.

Key dates

336BC Philip is murdered and Alexander comes to the Macedonian throne.

334BC Alexander invades Persia. He defeats the Persian governors of Asia Minor at the Battle of the River Granicus.

333BC Alexander defeats the Persians, led by King Darius, at the Battle of Issus.

332BC Siege and destruction of the city of Tyre in the Lebanon. Alexander conquers Egypt and founds city of Alexandria.

331BC Alexander defeats the Persians at the Battle of Gaugamela and becomes King of Persia.

327BC Alexander invades India.

326BC Alexander defeats the Indian King, Porus, at the Battle of the River Hydaspes.

323BC Alexander dies in Babylon.

Phrygia was a part of Asia Minor.

The Hellenistic World

For several hundred years after Alexander's† death, Greek culture and ideas dominated the countries of his empire. The period from 336-30BC is known as the Hellenistic Age, from the Greek word *Hellene*, which means "Greek".

When the news of Alexander's death reached Greece, many cities rebelled against the Macedonians. This began the Lamian War (323-322BC). The Greeks had some initial successes, but were defeated when the Macedonians were reinforced by soldiers returning from Asia.

Alexander was succeeded as ruler by his infant son and his half-brother, Philip Arrideus. Alexander's generals, known as the *Diadochi*, or "successors", governed the empire on behalf of the two kings. But the *Diadochi* began to divide the empire up between themselves and this led to wars over territory, lasting from 323-281BC.

This picture from a later Persian manuscript shows Alexander ascending to heaven.

The division of the empire

By 301BC, Alexander's mother, wife, son and half-brother had all been murdered in the struggle for power, and the empire had collapsed. After the Battle of Ipsus in 301BC, four kingdoms were established, with the rival *Diadochi* as kings. Finally, in 281BC, three kingdoms emerged (see map). They were ruled by the descendants of three of the *Diadochi*: Ptolemy†, Antigonas† and Seleucus†.

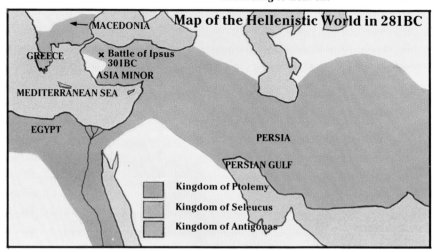

Map of the Hellenistic World in 281BC

MACEDONIA
GREECE
× Battle of Ipsus 301BC
ASIA MINOR
MEDITERRANEAN SEA
EGYPT
PERSIA
PERSIAN GULF

Kingdom of Ptolemy
Kingdom of Seleucus
Kingdom of Antigonas

Macedonia and Greece: 281-146BC

The Antigonids became the new Macedonian royal family. They ruled Greece from Macedonia, and controlled the country by keeping garrisons of soldiers in all the important cities. In 229BC Athens bribed its garrison to leave and became a neutral state. Although it never regained its political importance, Athens continued to be respected as the centre of Greek civilization.

During the third century BC, the Greek colonies in southern Italy became increasingly threatened by the Romans, who were expanding their territory throughout Italy (see opposite page). King Pyrrhus of Epirus went to the aid of the Greek colonists. He defeated the Romans twice, in 280BC and 279BC, but withdrew after a third battle in 275BC.

During the Hellenistic Period Greek craftsmen continued to produce many beautiful objects, such as this jewellery.

Gold pin, made in the 4th or 3rd century BC.

Gold earrings from the 1st century BC.

Gold diadem (headband), made in the 3rd century BC.

When the Romans occupied Greece in 147BC they stole many works of art from temples and houses and took them back to Italy.

Conflict with the Romans continued when King Philip V of Macedonia helped the Carthaginian general, Hannibal, in his fight against Rome. This provoked Roman reprisals, which led to three Macedonian Wars between the Antigonids and the Romans (215-205BC, 200-197BC and 179-168BC).

In 168BC the Macedonians were defeated at the Battle of Pydna. The Romans removed the Antigonids from power. After a Macedonian revolt in 147-146BC, the Romans put Macedonia and Greece under direct rule as provinces of the Roman Empire.

The Seleucids: 304-64BC

The Seleucids seized an enormous area of Alexander's empire, but it proved impossible to hold together. Despite inviting in Greek settlers, the Seleucids never had enough Greek manpower to control all their provinces. Gradually large areas began to break away, and by 180BC the Seleucids' territory had been greatly reduced (see map).

Wars with the Parthians, rebellions and disputed successions to the throne caused the gradual decay of the rest of the empire. It was finally ended in 64BC when the Roman general Pompey seized the Seleucid lands and they were incorporated into the Roman Empire.

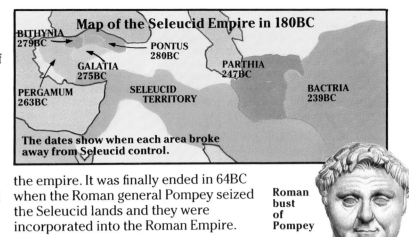

Map of the Seleucid Empire in 180BC

BITHYNIA 279BC

PONTUS 280BC

GALATIA 275BC

PARTHIA 247BC

PERGAMUM 263BC

SELEUCID TERRITORY

BACTRIA 239BC

The dates show when each area broke away from Seleucid control.

Roman bust of Pompey

The Ptolemaic empire: 323-30BC

Ptolemy was in many ways the most successful of the *Diadochi*. He had contented himself with taking just Egypt, and as a result was able to keep his kingdom intact. At the beginning of his reign, Ptolemy gained great prestige by having Alexander's body buried in splendour in Alexandria, which became the capital city of his empire.

Ptolemy and his successors governed Egypt from 323-30BC. The Ptolemies always preserved their Greek culture, and only the last ruler of the dynasty, Cleopatra VII, even learned the Egyptian language.

Egyptian carving of Ptolemy.

Confusion over the succession and increasing Roman involvement in Egyptian affairs finally destroyed the Ptolemy dynasty. Queen Cleopatra VII and her Roman husband, Mark Antony, were defeated by the Romans at the Battle of Actium in 31BC. Egypt, the last remaining Hellenistic Kingdom, became a Roman province in 30BC.

The Ptolemies introduced many Greek things to Egypt. This mosaic shows an Egyptian warship, which was based on a Greek trireme†.

The Romans

The Romans developed from a tribe who migrated from central Europe and settled around the river Tiber in Italy in c.1000BC. By about 250BC the Romans controlled most of Italy. After this they started to expand their territory abroad and, thanks to their military efficiency, soon built up a large empire (see map).

The arch of Constantine in Rome

The Romans eventually conquered all the Hellenistic kingdoms and were greatly influenced by the Greek ideas they met there. They adopted many aspects of Greek life, such as architecture, literature, religion and social customs. This helped to keep Greek culture alive, even after the end of the Hellenistic Period.

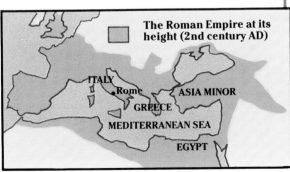

The Roman Empire at its height (2nd century AD)

ITALY

Rome

ASIA MINOR

GREECE

MEDITERRANEAN SEA

EGYPT

Key dates

323-322BC The Greek states rebel against the Macedonians in the Lamian War, but are defeated.

323-281BC Wars of the *Diadochi*, ending in the establishment of three *Diadochi* kingdoms.

275BC Greek colonies in southern Italy pass to the Romans after the defeat of King Pyrrhus of Epirus.

168BC King Perseus of Macedonia is defeated by the Romans at the Battle of Pydna. The Macedonian monarchy is abolished.

147-146BC The Romans suppress a Macedonian revolt. Macedonia and Greece become provinces of the Roman Empire.

64BC The Seleucid empire is conquered by the Roman general, Pompey, and becomes a Roman province.

31-30BC Cleopatra VII of Egypt is defeated by the Romans at the Battle of Actium and Egypt becomes a Roman province.

Learning

Early Greeks used stories about the gods to answer questions about how the world worked or the purpose of life. However, in the 6th century BC some people started to look for new, more practical explanations. To obtain this knowledge, they asked questions and made observations and calculations about the world around them. The Greeks called these scholars *philosophers*, which means "lovers of knowledge".

Today we think of philosophy as the study of the nature of the universe and of human life. However, early Greek philosophers also studied many other subjects, such as biology, mathematics, astronomy and geography.

Scientists and inventors

By observing how things worked, Greek philosophers were able to make many new scientific discoveries, some of which have provided the foundations of modern science.

The astronomer Aristarchus deduced that the Earth revolved on its axis and that it moved around the Sun. This idea was not generally accepted because he could not produce evidence to prove it.

A scholar called Archimedes† discovered an important law of physics. One day he got into a bath and the water overflowed. From this he worked out that an object always displaces its own volume of water.

Thales of Miletus was able to calculate the height of one of the Egyptian pyramids by measuring its shadow. He is also said to have been able to predict an eclipse of the Sun.

Anaximander worked out that much of the land had once been covered in water. He also believed that humans had not appeared on Earth in their present form, but had developed from an earlier creature, perhaps a fish. Another scholar, Xenophanes, examined fossils and discovered that they were the remains of plants and animals preserved in rock.

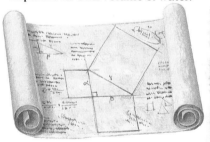

Greek scholars, such as Pythagoras†, Euclid† and Archimedes worked out many basic rules of mathematics. They devised theorems which are still used in geometry. These include Pythagoras' theorem on triangles and the use of pi in working out the circumference or area of a circle.

Another astronomer, Anaxagoras†, realized that the Moon did not produce light itself, but reflected the light of the Sun. He also worked out that eclipses were caused by the Moon passing between the Earth and the Sun and blocking the light.

The Museum

In the Hellenistic Period a temple to the Muses (see page 54) was built at Alexandria in Egypt. It was called the Museum. Scholars from all over the Greek world worked there. The Museum also had a library which contained every important Greek book, as well as translations of many foreign books.

We know that engineers at the Museum invented some interesting devices, many of which used water or steam power. However, some of these machines were not very practical and were never widely used. Two of the more useful ones are shown here.

Many inventors at the Museum tried to produce effective new weapons. These were mostly catapults and crossbows. The Greek designs remained in use for many years.

Crossbow

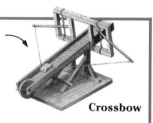

Archimedes built a device which raised water from one level to another. It was in the form of a large screw. Water rose through the screw as it was turned. Pumps like this are still used in parts of Africa today.

Political and moral philosophers

Greek philosophers also examined questions such as how people should behave or what would be the ideal political system. Their ideas were very influential and form the basis of the subject we now call philosophy. Some of the most important thinkers are shown below.

Pythagoras, a mathematician ▶ from Samos, founded a sacred community in Italy. He was interested in what happened to people after they died. He taught that, at death, the soul passed into the body of another creature and so was born again.

Socrates† thought that people would ▶ behave well if they knew what good behaviour was. He challenged people to think about truth, good and evil. He became very unpopular with some Athenians. Finally they charged him with disobeying religious laws and he was forced to kill himself.

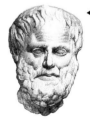

Socrates never wrote down his ideas. They were reported by his pupils, one of whom was Plato†. In his own work, Plato tried to find the ideal way of governing a state and set out detailed rules about how this could ◀ be done.

◀ Aristotle† was born in 384BC and was a pupil of Plato. He had a wide knowledge of politics and science. He too was interested in man and society, and finding the ideal way to run a city state. One of his pupils was Alexander the Great†.

In the 4th century BC, Diogenes ▶ founded the school of philosophers known as Cynics. He had no respect for the rules and regulations of society and lived very simply. At one point his home was a large storage jar. He attacked dishonesty and excessive wealth.

The Stoic philosophers ▶ were named after the *stoa* † (porch) where their founder, Xenon, taught. He believed that if people acted naturally they would behave well, because their nature was controlled by the gods. Xenon thought that people should live calmly and reasonably.

Historians

When the earliest Greeks wanted to know about the past, they relied on the stories of gods and heroes that had been handed down to them. They had little interest in the past of other peoples. However, in the 6th century BC when they were threatened by the Persians, the Greeks needed to know more about their opponents. Writers started to gather facts about the Persians and other foreigners. However, these accounts were not always very accurate. It was not until the 5th century BC that more reliable material about the Greeks and other peoples was recorded.

Herodotus† is considered to be the first true historian and is often known as the "Father of History". He wrote a history of the Persian Wars after interviewing many survivors and their families to find out what had happened. He also travelled widely and wrote about peoples such as the Persians and Egyptians.

Another important historian was Thucydides†. He wrote a history of the Peloponnesian War, which is regarded as one of the finest early works of history. Thucydides fought in the war himself and he also interviewed other people who had taken part.

Xenophon† was an army commander, and fought with the Spartans in the Persian Wars. He wrote about many subjects, including the Persian Wars, a history of Greece, military tactics, politics and the care and breeding of horses.

Medicine

Many Greek doctors were priests of Asclepius, the god of healing (see box). By 420BC the cult of Asclepius had been established in Athens, where a festival called the *Epidauria* was held in his honour. Soon there were temples to him all over the Greek world. One of the most important was at Epidaurus, in the Peloponnese.

This reconstruction shows part of the temple complex at Epidaurus.

Asclepius

According to legend, Asclepius was the son of the god Apollo. He was brought up by a *centaur* (a creature that was half man, half horse), who taught him medicine. The goddess Athene gave Asclepius two bottles of magic blood. The blood in one bottle would kill anything, that in the other would bring the dead back to life. Asclepius brought so many people back from the dead that Pluto, the god of the Underworld, complained to Zeus. Zeus was angry with Asclepius and killed him. However, he later relented, brought Asclepius back to life and made him a god.

This statue shows Asclepius with a snake. The snake was the symbol of medicine, and is often still used in this way today.

Religious cures

When they were ill, people visited one of the temples of Asclepius. There priests offered both ordinary medicines and the hope of a miraculous cure. Sick people first had to perform sacrifices and purification ceremonies.

Then they were allowed to sleep for a night in the god's temple. It was thought that Asclepius would heal them while they slept. Sometimes he might appear in a dream to reveal what treatment would cure them.

People who were cured left offerings to Asclepius. This was often a model of the part of the body that had been cured. This relief† shows a man making an offering to Asclepius of a model of a leg.

Developments in medical practice

Later, some doctors adopted a more scientific approach to medicine. They tried to use practical cures rather than religious ones, though they still respected Asclepius. The founder of this movement was a doctor called Hippocrates† of Kos, who is thought to have lived from about 460-377BC. His followers opened schools where the new type of medicine was taught.

The new doctors did not believe that illness was a punishment from the gods. Instead they searched for the causes of disease and tried to find out how the body worked. This relief shows a doctor examining a patient to find out what is wrong with him.

Doctors normally prescribed herbal medicines, a special diet, rest or gentle exercise. Sometimes they removed some blood, as it was thought to contain the disease. This vase shows a doctor taking blood from a patient's arm.

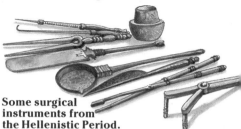

Some surgical instruments from the Hellenistic Period.

As there were no anaesthetics, operations were extremely painful and dangerous. Even if they survived the treatment, patients often died of infected wounds. Doctors therefore tried to avoid operations whenever possible.

Map of Ancient Greece

This map shows Ancient Greece and the surrounding area. All the cities and regions which have been mentioned earlier in the book are marked on this map. The names of regions or countries are written in capital letters. Cities are written in small letters and their positions are marked by dots.

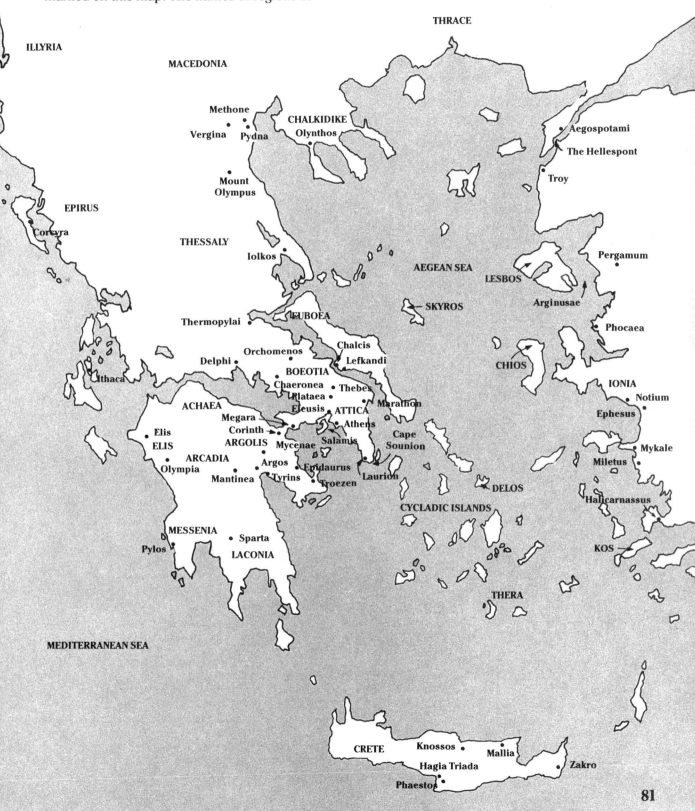

THRACE

ILLYRIA

MACEDONIA

Methone
Vergina   Pydna
CHALKIDIKE
Olynthos

Aegospotami
The Hellespont
Troy

Mount
Olympus

EPIRUS
Corcyra

THESSALY
Iolkos

AEGEAN SEA

Pergamum

LESBOS
SKYROS
Arginusae

Phocaea

Thermopylai
EUBOEA

CHIOS

Delphi   Orchomenos
Chalcis
Lefkandi
BOEOTIA
Chaeronea   Thebes
Plataea
Eleusis   Marathon
ATTICA
Athens
Megara
Corinth →
Salamis
Cape
Sounion
ARGOLIS   Mycenae
ACHAEA
Elis
ELIS
ARCADIA   Argos   Epidaurus
Olympia   Tyrins   Laurion
Mantinea   Troezen

Ithaca

IONIA
Notium
Ephesus

Mykale
Miletus

Halicarnassus

DELOS
CYCLADIC ISLANDS

KOS

MESSENIA
Sparta
Pylos
LACONIA

THERA

MEDITERRANEAN SEA

CRETE   Knossos   Mallia
Hagia Triada   Zakro
Phaestos

81

Greek myths and legends

The earliest Greeks had many myths – stories about gods and goddesses – which they told to explain the world around them. Later, many legends developed which described the lives and deeds of famous heroes in Greek history.

Below are some of the most important Greek myths and legends. Important names appear in bold type to make the main characters easier to identify. You can also read more about the most important gods and goddesses on pages 64-65.

Demeter and Persephone

Demeter, the goddess of crops and harvests, had a beautiful daughter called **Persephone**. **Pluto**, the god of the Underworld, caught sight of Persephone one day and fell in love with her. He had been unable to find a wife, as nobody wanted to live with him in the Underworld where the sun never shone. So he decided to kidnap Persephone and make her his queen. He drove by in his chariot, seized her and carried her off.

Zeus intervenes

Demeter was very upset when she realized her daughter had disappeared. She neglected the plants and trees to look for Persephone. When she found out what had happened, she pleaded with **Zeus** to make Pluto release her daughter. Zeus promised to help her, because no crops would grow and people were starving. So he decreed that Pluto should let Persephone go, on condition that she had not tasted the food of the dead while she had been in the Underworld.

Persephone returns

Persephone had been so miserable that she had not eaten anything, but just before he released her, Pluto persuaded her to taste six pomegranate seeds from his garden. So Zeus decided that she could return to Earth, but would have to spend six months of each year with Pluto in the Underworld, one for each seed she had eaten. Persephone returned to her mother, who was delighted. The crops grew again and it was spring. But after that, for half of every year, Persephone went back to live with Pluto. Demeter became so sad that all the crops died, and it was winter once more.

Theseus

Theseus was the son of **Aegeus**, the king of Athens. As a young man, Aegeus travelled to a place called Troezene and fell in love with a princess called **Aethra**. However he had to return to Athens, and could not take Aethra with him, even though she was pregnant. Before he left, he buried his sword and sandals under a stone. Aegeus told Aethra that if she had a son, when he grew up he should lift the stone and take the sword and sandals to Athens, where he would be introduced to the people as Aegeus' son and heir. Aethra gave birth to a son, and named him **Theseus**.

Theseus travels to Athens

When he was old enough, Theseus found the sandals and sword and set off to Athens to find his father. When he arrived, he went to meet his father, but Aegeus' wife, **Medea**, saw him first. She knew he had come for his inheritance, and wanted to stop him. She handed Aegeus some wine to give to the stranger, but she had secretly poisoned it.

Aegeus recognizes Theseus

When Aegeus saw Theseus' sword and sandals he knew at once who he was, and moved to embrace him. As he did so he dropped the cup of wine. The contents fell on a dog at the king's feet, and killed it instantly. Aegeus then knew that Medea had tried to poison his son. She fled from Athens and never returned.

Theseus and the Minotaur

Some time after Theseus arrived in Athens, the Athenians became anxious and unhappy. When Theseus asked why, he was told that once a year the Athenians were forced to send young men and women to the island of Crete, as food for a monster called the **Minotaur**. It was half man, half bull, and had been born to the wife of **Minos**, the King of Crete (see pages 4 and 9). It lived in a maze called the Labyrinth, which was so confusing that people who entered it never found a way out. The Minotaur ate people who were thrown into the maze.

The voyage to Crete

Theseus volunteered to join the victims in order to kill the monster. Aegeus tried to persuade his son not to go, but Theseus boarded the ship, which had black sails. He promised that if he succeeded, he would change the sails to white ones on the return journey, so that Aegeus would know the outcome as soon as possible.

Into the Labyrinth

When Theseus got to Crete, Minos' daughter **Ariadne** fell in love with him. She gave him a sword to kill the Minotaur, and a ball of thread. Theseus tied one end of the thread to the entrance of the Labyrinth, and went inside. He found and killed the Minotaur, then followed the thread back outside. Ariadne, Theseus and his friends then fled from Crete.

Ariadne is abandoned

On the way back to Athens, they visited the island of Naxos. By this time Theseus was growing tired of Ariadne. While she was asleep, he called his friends back to the ship. They set sail, abandoning her. The gods disapproved, and punished Theseus by making him forget to hoist the white sails. Aegeus, watching from the shore for the ship, saw the black sails and thought that his son was dead. In his grief he threw himself off a cliff. Ever since, the sea where he died has been called the Aegean.

Theseus travels again

When Theseus heard about his father he was griefstricken. To help him forget his sadness, he set out to travel again. He went to the land of a race of warrior women called the **Amazons**, and married the Amazon queen. They returned to Athens, where a son, **Hippolytus**, was born. Shortly after this, the Amazons invaded Athens to take their queen back, but she was killed in a battle.

Phaedra

Theseus married again. His new wife, **Phaedra**, was jealous of Hippolytus and wanted to get rid of him. She told Theseus that Hippolytus had attacked her. The king was very angry, and asked **Poseidon** to punish his son. As Hippolytus was riding on the beach, Poseidon sent a huge wave to scare his horses. The horses bolted and Hippolytus was killed.

The death of Theseus

Phaedra was overcome with remorse. She confessed that she had lied, and then hanged herself. Theseus grew bitter after all these misfortunes, and became a very stern ruler. The Athenians turned against him and banished him to the island of Scyros, where he was murdered. Later Theseus' bones were returned to Athens, where a temple was built in his honour.

Oedipus

Oedipus was the son of **Laius** and **Jocasta**, the King and Queen of Thebes in Boeotia. When he was born, they asked the priests of Apollo to foretell the child's fate. They were horrified to be told that Oedipus was destined to murder his father and marry his mother. To prevent this, Laius made one of his servants take Oedipus away and kill him. The servant did not murder the child, but left him outside to die. A shepherd found the baby and took him to Corinth, where the king and queen adopted him and brought him up as their own son.

Oedipus consults the Oracle

When he grew up, Oedipus went to Delphi to ask the Oracle (see page 68) what the future held. He too was told that he would kill his father and marry his mother. Thinking the king and queen of Corinth were his parents, he left Corinth, vowing never to return.

Oedipus' journey

While travelling he came to a crossroads, where he saw a man being driven in a chariot. The driver called to him to make way, but Oedipus did not move. He was used to being treated as a prince, and would not accept orders. A fight began, and Oedipus killed the driver, the man and his servants. He did not know it, but the man was Laius. The first part of the prophecy had come true.

Oedipus and the Sphinx

Oedipus continued towards Thebes. Near the city he encountered a monster called the **Sphinx** that was terrorizing the area. She sat by the city gates, and would not let people past without asking them a riddle. When they could not answer, she ate them. No-one had yet got past the Sphinx, and no-one dared to attack her.

The Sphinx's riddle

Oedipus was still so sad about having left Corinth that he did not care whether he lived or died. He approached the Sphinx to try and guess the answer to her riddle. This is what she asked him: What has four legs in the morning, two at mid-day, and three in the evening, and is weakest when it has most legs?

Oedipus realized the answer was a human being, who crawls, then walks, then, when old, uses a stick for support. The Sphinx was so angry at being defeated that she killed herself. The happy Thebans made Oedipus their king, and he married the Queen, Jocasta.

The plague

All went well for some years, but then Thebes was hit by a plague. Many people died, and the people turned again to Oedipus to help them. He sent messengers to consult the Oracle at Delphi, who declared that the plague would only cease if Laius' murderers were found and punished.

Oedipus learns the truth

Messengers were sent to find out who had committed the murder. They returned with evidence that it had been Oedipus. The servant who had taken the baby to the hillside confessed that he had not killed the child, but had simply left him to die. Enquiries in Corinth confirmed that the baby had been adopted there. Oedipus realized that the prophecy had come true. Without knowing it he had murdered his father and married his mother. When she discovered what had happened, Jocasta killed herself. Oedipus blinded himself with her brooch, fled from Thebes, and died, ruined, at Colonnus near Athens.

The curse of the family of Atreus

Atreus became king of Mycenae when he married **Aerope**, a Mycenaean princess. But it was said that Atreus was subject to several curses, which caused him and his family great suffering and misery.

Tantalus offends the gods

Atreus' grandfather, **Tantalus**, had been a friend of **Zeus**, and was allowed to eat with the gods. But he offended them by stealing their food and giving it to his friends on Earth. Then he asked the gods to a banquet, and tested them to see if they truly were all-powerful. He killed his son, **Pelops**, and served him up at the feast, though it was forbidden to eat human flesh. The gods knew at once what had happened. Zeus condemned Tantalus to eternal torment in the Underworld, and put a curse on his family.

Pelops returns from the dead

Zeus brought Pelops back to life. When the boy grew up he fell in love with a princess, **Hippodamia**, and asked to marry her. Her father, King **Oenomaus**, had been told by fortune tellers that he would be killed by his son-in-law, and so wished to stop anyone from marrying his daughter. He challenged her suitors to a chariot race, stating that the loser would be executed. The god **Poseidon** lent Pelops some of his horses. In addition, Pelops bribed the king's charioteer, **Myrtilus**, promising him a reward if he would sabotage the king's chariot.

The chariot race

Oenomaus was killed in a crash during the race, and Pelops escaped with Hippodamia and Myrtilus. Instead of rewarding the charioteer, however, Pelops murdered him. As he died, Myrtilus placed a curse on Pelops.

A third curse

Later, Atreus himself was the victim of a curse. He found out that his wife had been seduced by his brother **Thyestes**. He took revenge by killing all but one of Thyestes' sons. Thyestes then put a curse on his brother.

The curses are fulfilled

The curses were fulfilled during the reign of **Agamemnon**, Atreus' son. **Menelaus**, Agamemnon's brother, had married **Helen**, the Queen of Sparta. Helen was so beautiful that all the Greek kings had fallen in love with her, but they had been made to swear that they would help the man she married if anyone tried to steal her away. But the goddess of love, **Aphrodite**, had promised a Trojan Prince called **Paris** that he could marry Helen. He went to Sparta, where Helen fell in love with him, and they ran away to live at Troy.

Agamemnon plots his revenge

Agamemnon was angry about Helen's treatment of Menelaus. He reminded the other kings of their oath and organized an expedition to Troy to bring Helen back. To get good winds for the sea journey he even sacrificed his daughter **Iphigenia**. The war against Troy lasted ten years (see pages 14-15) before the Greeks won and Agamemnon returned home.

Agamemnon is murdered

Meanwhile, Agamemnon's wife, **Clytemnestra**, was angered by the sacrifice of Iphigenia, and by her husband's long absence. She fell in love with **Aegistus**, her husband's cousin and enemy, and married him. She pretended to welcome Agamemnon when he came home, but then murdered him. She and Aegistus then ruled Mycenae.

Revenge, and the end of the curse

Agamemnon's son **Orestes** found out what had happened and took revenge, murdering Clytemnestra and Aegistus. By killing his own mother, Orestes had committed a terrible crime. He was driven mad by the **Furies**, goddesses with dogs' heads and bats' wings who tormented murderers. Finally the gods intervened, seeing that Orestes had suffered enough. They cleansed Orestes of his guilt, and ended the curse. Orestes became king of Mycenae.

Two poems by Homer

The earliest surviving examples of Greek literature are two poems by Homer†, the *Iliad* and the *Odyssey*. Homer only passed his poems on by word of mouth, but when writing was reintroduced in Greece, later scholars and poets wrote them down. For the Greeks, Homer's work was a magnificent source of inspiration about religion and history. For people of later civilizations, the *Iliad* and the *Odyssey* have provided a wealth of information about Homer's world.

The *Iliad*

The *Iliad* takes place during the last few weeks of the Trojan War (see page 14). It concerns an argument between the hero **Achilles** and the leader of the Greek forces, **Agamemnon**. Agamemnon stole a slave-girl from Achilles, who, insulted, withdrew from the fighting. Without him, the Greeks were downhearted and suffered terrible losses. To boost the troops' morale, Achilles' friend **Patroclus** put on Achilles' armour and went into battle. Thinking he was Achilles, a Trojan warrior called **Hector** killed him.

Achilles, full of remorse, returned to the battlefield and killed Hector. He dragged the body round the walls of Troy behind his chariot. Hector's father, **Priam**, paid a ransom to Achilles, who finally returned the body. Hector was given a hero's funeral.

The poem contains many episodes about other heroes and their deeds. The human events are mirrored by episodes about the gods and goddesses, who each take sides in the dispute.

The *Odyssey*

The *Odyssey* tells the story of another hero, **Odysseus**, who suggested the trick of the wooden horse (see page 14). After the Trojan War, Odysseus tried to return home to Ithaca, where his wife **Penelope** was besieged by suitors. They thought Odysseus was dead, and wanted to marry her. They insisted that she chose one of them as a husband.

Much of the *Odyssey* tells the story of Odysseus'

journey home, and of the many dangers he encountered. He had to slay the one-eyed monster **Cyclops**, and survive many shipwrecks. He also escaped from the **Sirens**, creatures whose singing lured ships to crash on to the rocks, and from **Circe**, a witch who turned men into animals.

When he reached Ithaca, the goddess **Athene** disguised him as a beggar, to help him return to his house unnoticed. Penelope had organized an archery competition for her suitors, saying she would marry the winner. Odysseus, still disguised, took part in the competition and won. He then killed the other competitors. Finally Penelope recognized him and the couple were reunited.

Who was who in Ancient Greece

Below is a list of the important people mentioned in this book, with details of their lives and works. If a person's name appears in **bold type** in the text of an entry, that person also has his or her own entry in this list.

Aeschylus (c.525BC-455BC).   Writer of tragic plays. He wrote about 90 plays, but only seven survive. Most of his tragedies were stories about the gods and the heroes. His most famous work is the *Orestia*, a group of three plays about King Agamemnon and his family (see page 83). Aeschylus is regarded as the founder of Greek tragedy. He was the first writer to use more than one actor, making dialogue and action on stage possible.

Alcibiades (c.450BC-404BC).   Athenian politician. He was a pupil of **Socrates** and the ward of **Pericles**, who was a close relative. In 420BC he was elected *strategos†*. During the Peloponnesian War, he persuaded the Athenians to send troops to Sicily (see page 63) and was appointed one of the leaders of the expedition. However, he was recalled to face a charge of having mutilated many statues in Athens with a group of aristocratic friends. Instead he fled to Sparta where he advised the Spartans how to fight their war against Athens. In 407BC he was recalled to Athens and re-elected. However, he was held responsible for the Athenian defeat at the Battle of Notium, and retired. He was assassinated in Persia.

Alexander the Great (356BC-323BC).   Macedonian king and military leader. He was a pupil of **Aristotle**, and learned military tactics as a soldier in the army of his father, **Philip of Macedonia**. In 336BC Philip was murdered, and Alexander became king at the age of 20. He was a military genius, and, after taking control of Greece and the areas to the north, in 334BC he began an invasion of Asia. Eventually he conquered the largest empire in the Ancient World (see pages 74-75). Alexander married a Persian princess called Roxane. He died of a fever at Babylon, aged only 32.

Anaxagoras (c.500BC-c.428BC).   Philosopher. He spent most of his life in Athens, and was a friend of **Pericles**. He wrote a book called *On Nature* in which he tried to explain how the universe worked. This book influenced many later philosophers. In the scientific field, Anaxagoras worked out that the Sun was a mass of flaming material and that the Moon reflected its light. He was also the first person to explain a solar eclipse.

Antigonas II.   Macedonian king. He ruled from 279BC to 239BC. As king of Macedonia he also ruled Greece itself, and was one of the most powerful leaders of the Hellenistic World (see pages 76-77). His successors ruled until 146BC, when Macedonia and Greece were conquered by the Romans.

Archimedes (c.287-212BC).   Mathematician, astronomer and inventor. He studied at the Museum in Alexandria (see page 78) and then lived in Syracuse. He invented a type of pulley and a device for raising water. He also discovered an important law of physics – that a body displaces its own volume of water.

Aristides (c.520BC-c.467BC).   Athenian politician and general. He came from an aristocratic family. Aristides was a prominent leader at the time of the Persian Wars and was a *strategos†* at the Battle of Marathon. He was ostracized† in 482BC, but was recalled a year later and took part in the battles of Salamis and Plataea (see page 41). Aristides also helped to set up the Delian League.

Aristophanes (5th century BC-c.385BC).   Athenian writer of comic plays. He wrote about 40 comedies, of which eleven survive. Some of these make fun of the political events of the time. Many of his works won prizes at the Athens Theatre Festival. His most famous plays are *The Wasps*, *The Birds* and *The Frogs*.

Aristotle (384BC-322BC).   Athenian philosopher. He studied with **Plato** in Athens, then travelled around the eastern Mediterranean. After spending three years as the tutor of **Alexander the Great**, he returned to Athens in 335BC. He set up a school, the Lyceum, but after Alexander's death he was charged with impiety and fled to Euboea. His writings cover many different subjects, such as poetry, political life, and various philosophical theories. Some of his most famous works are *Poetics*, *Politica* and *Metaphysica*.

Aspasia (born c.465BC).   Wife of **Pericles**. She came from Miletus, and was never properly accepted by many Athenians. She was often mocked by Pericles' enemies, and by writers of comedies. However she was very beautiful and well educated, and was highly regarded by **Socrates** and his friends. In 431BC she was prosecuted, but acquitted.

Cimon (late 6th century BC-c.450BC).   Athenian soldier and statesman. He was the son of **Miltiades**, and a sworn enemy of the Persians. After the Greek victory over the Persians at the battles of Salamis and Plataea (see page 41), Cimon led expeditions to free the Greek islands from Persian rule. He was responsible for several later victories against the Persians. In 462BC he persuaded Athens to support Sparta (see page 63). When the Spartans refused Athenian help Cimon's prestige suffered and he was ostracized† in 461BC. Later he was recalled, and negotiated the 5-year peace with Sparta. He led an expedition to Cyprus, where he died.

Cleisthenes (lived 6th century BC).   Athenian politician. He was a member of the Athenian aristocracy, and took power in Athens after the overthrow of the tyrant Hippias. In 580BC he introduced reforms that led to the political system known as democracy† (see pages 60-61). He also introduced ostracism† in the city. **Pericles** was his nephew.

Draco (lived 7th century BC).   Athenian politician. In 621BC he was appointed to improve the Athenian legal system. He favoured public trials so that people could see that justice had been done. He based his reforms on existing laws, but made them much more severe, and introduced the death penalty for many minor crimes. The Athenians became unhappy with such severe laws, and the system was later reformed again by **Solon**.

Euclid (lived c.300BC).   Mathematician. He worked in Alexandria, and wrote several books about mathematics and geometry. His most famous book was *Elements*, part of which sums up the teachings of the mathematicians who worked before him. Several of his theories and discoveries remain in use today.

Euripides (c.485BC-406BC).   Athenian writer of tragic plays. He wrote over 90 plays, of which we know the titles of 80; 19 of them have survived. Among the most famous are *Medea*, *The Trojan Women* and *Orestes*. He won five first prizes at the Athens Theatre Festival. Later he moved to the court of King Archelaus of Macedonia, where he died.

Herodotus (c.484BC-420BC).   Historian. He was born in Helicarnassus in Ionia. He visited Egypt, the Black Sea, Babylon and Cyrene, then lived on Samos. Later he moved to Athens, but he finally settled in Thurii in southern Italy. Herodotus is known as "the Father of History". He wrote a history of the Greek people which centred around the Persian Wars. It also included information on many other, very varied subjects. Herodotus was one of the first writers to compare historical facts and to see them as a sequence of linked events.

Hesiod (lived ?8th century BC).   Boeotian poet. He owned a farm at Ascra in Boeotia. He claimed that the Muses (see page 54) visited him one day on Mount Helicon and gave him the gift of poetry. His most famous book is *Works and Days*, which includes practical details of farming, a calendar of lucky and unlucky days, and an explanation of religious ceremonies. He is also said to have written *The Theogony*, an account of the Greek gods and goddesses and their relationships.

Hippocrates (c.460BC-c.377BC).   Doctor and writer on medicine. His teachings became the basis of medical practice throughout the ancient world (see page 80). Unlike many earlier Greek doctors, he based his work on close observations of his patients, rather than on religious rituals. His writings discuss many aspects of medical practice, including the way a doctor should behave, and the effect of the environment on disease and illness. Hippocrates lived on the island of Kos, where he founded an important medical school.

Homer (lived ?9th century BC).   Poet. Very little is known about him. He was a bard (see page 14) who recited his poems. For many years his work was passed on by word of mouth. Eventually fragments of it were written down by other poets and historians centuries after his death. According to tradition he came from the island of Chios, and may have been blind. His poems *The Iliad* and *The Odyssey* are accounts of events during and after the Trojan War (see pages 14-15).

Miltiades (c.550BC-c.489BC).   Athenian soldier and politician, father of **Cimon**. He was sent by the tyrant† Hippias to the Chersonese to make sure that the Athenians kept control of the route through to the Black Sea. Later he fought for the Persians, but joined the Ionian revolt (see page 40) in 500BC. When the revolt was defeated he had to flee to Athens. He led the Athenian forces at the Battle of Marathon, which the Greeks won, largely thanks to Miltiades' superior military skills. Later he led the Athenian fleet in an unsuccessful expedition to Paros, where he was wounded. As a result of this failure he returned to Athens, where he was tried and fined a huge sum of money. He died shortly after the trial.

Myron (lived 5th century BC).   Sculptor. He worked in Athens between about 460 and 440BC. His most famous statues included one of the runner Ladas, and one of a man throwing a discus (see page 46).

Peisistratus (c.590BC-527BC).   Athenian politician. In 546BC, after two earlier attempts to seize power, he declared himself tyrant† of Athens (see page 21). Under his rule Athens prospered. He reorganized public finances, and spent public money on roads and a good water supply. He also rebuilt and improved much of Athens, and art and literature were encouraged. Athenian trade with the rest of Greece also improved because Peisistratus was an excellent diplomat and wanted good relations with other areas. He died while still in power.

Pericles (early 5th century BC-429BC).   Athenian statesman and general. He was a member of the aristocratic Alcmaeonid family, and became the most famous and powerful politician of his day. He was elected *strategos*† every year from 443BC to 429BC, and was such a powerful speaker that he was nearly always able to swing public opinion his way. He was responsible for the rebuilding of the Acropolis, the construction of the Long Walls (see page 62), and for refining the Athenian democratic system. He dictated the Athenian policy during the early stages of the Peloponnesian War. In 430BC he was charged with stealing public funds and fined a huge sum of money. He was still elected strategos the following year, but died in the plague that hit Athens.

Pheidias (c.500BC-c.425BC).   Athenian sculptor. He worked as a painter before becoming a sculptor. He mostly used bronze, but was best known for his cult statues in ivory and gold. He made the frieze around the Parthenon and the statue of Athene there, as well as the statue of Zeus at Olympus. He was accused of taking the gold given to him for work on the Parthenon, but escaped and went to work at Olympus. Later he was again charged with embezzlement, and died in prison.

Philip of Macedonia (c.382BC-336BC).   Macedonian king and military leader. He began ruling Macedonia in 359BC (see pages 72-73). He reorganized the army, and showed great skill as a military commander and diplomat. Within 25 years Philip had united the country, extended the frontiers, and made Macedonia into the greatest military power of its day. Philip married a princess called Olympias, and they had a son, **Alexander**. He was assassinated in 336BC; it is possible that his wife and son were involved in the murder plot.

Pindar (c.518BC-c.438BC).   Athenian poet. He was born in Boeotia, and travelled to Athens at an early age. He was a friend of **Aeschylus**, and quickly became known as a poet. Ancient scholars divided his many poems into 17 books according to themes and styles. Some celebrate victors at games, some are odes to tyrants, and a few other fragments have survived. Many later writers described him as the greatest Greek poet.

Plato (c.429BC-347BC).   Athenian philosopher. He was a member of an aristocratic Athenian family, and a pupil of **Socrates**. After Socrates died, Plato fled to Megara, then lived in Syracuse. Later he returned to Athens, where he wrote *The Apology*, an answer to Socrates' enemies. His ideas for the running of an ideal state were set out in his books *The Republic* and *The Laws*. He founded a school on the outskirts of Athens, in a grove called the Academy which gave the school its name. The school was famous throughout the ancient world, and continued for centuries after Plato's death. It was closed in AD529 by the Roman Emperor Justinian, who thought it was politically dangerous. Plato's ideas have remained influential to the present day.

Praxiteles (born c.390BC).   Athenian sculptor. Little is known about his life, except that he worked in Athens. His sculpture of the goddess Aphrodite (see page 47) is the first known statue of the female nude. Praxiteles also made sculptures of the gods Hermes, Eros and Apollo.

Ptolemy I.   Macedonian general, later King of Egypt. He took over Egypt after the death of **Alexander the Great** in 323BC. He and his successors ruled successfully until Egypt was conquered by the Romans in 30BC.

Pythagoras (c.580BC-late 6th century BC). Philosopher and mathematician. He may have travelled in Egypt and the East. Later he founded a school at Croton in southern Italy. Nothing has survived of his theories, but we know about his teachings from contemporary descriptions. He thought that after people died their souls lived on in other beings. He also developed many geometrical theories (see page 78).

Sappho (born c.612BC).   Poetess. She was born on the island of Lesbos, but probably left there to travel to Sicily. For a time she ran a school for girls. It is said that she wrote nine books of poetry, but only fragments survive. Sappho was considered one of the greatest Greek poets. She died in the middle of the 6th century BC.

Seleucus I.   Macedonian general, later Middle Eastern king. In 304BC he seized a vast area of the empire of **Alexander the Great**, and became one of the three main rulers of the Hellenistic World (see pages 76-77). But the empire was too big to hold together and it was eventually conquered by the Romans in 64BC.

Socrates (c.469BC-399BC).   Athenian philosopher. He wrote no books, but taught his pupils by word of mouth, discussing points of philosophy with them and questioning accepted opinions. Socrates and his pupils pointed out weak points in the government, and in people's beliefs. This made them very unpopular with Athenian politicians. Eventually his enemies charged him with impiety and corrupting the young. He was sentenced to death by drinking poison. We know about Socrates' ideas (see page 79) because they were written down by some of his pupils, including **Plato**.

Solon (c.640BC-558BC).   Athenian politician. He became *archon*† in about 594BC, and quickly passed many new laws (see page 21). These included bringing debtors back from exile, and the cancellation of many debts. He set up a new court to which people could appeal if they thought they had been wrongly tried, and also reformed the way the government took decisions. Solon encouraged craftsmen from other parts of Greece to come to Athens, and granted them Athenian citizenship. By making the Athenians use the same money as other Greek states he also encouraged the development of trade and industry.

Sophocles (c.496BC-405BC).   Athenian writer of tragic plays. He wrote 123 plays, of which we know the titles of 110, but only seven survive. The most famous are *Antigone*, *Oedipus Tyrannus* and *Electra*. He won many prizes at the Athens Theatre Festival. Sophocles was among the first to write plays with more than two characters, and one of the first to use stage scenery. Before him, plays had concentrated on myths and the affairs of the gods. His plays, though still based on myths, were written from the viewpoint of the human characters.

Themistocles (c.524BC-459BC).   Athenian statesman. He was *strategos*† at the Battle of Marathon (see page 40) and persuaded the Athenians to build up their navy. In 480-479BC he organised resistance to the Persians. His strategy helped the Athenians to win the Battle of Salamis (see page 41). Later he organized the rebuilding of the walls of Athens in 479-478BC. Around 471BC he was ostracized† and fled to Argos. He was accused of treason. Then he fled to Asia Minor where the Persians, grateful to him for his part in negotiating peace with Athens, made him governor of three cities.

Thucydides (c.460BC-396BC).   Athenian historian. In 424BC he was elected *strategos*†, but he was held responsible for a military defeat and was ostracized†. He did not return to Athens for 20 years. Thucydides wrote an account of the Peloponnesian War which is considered to be one of the first history books. As well as describing the battles and political events, it gives details of life in Athens and elsewhere.

Xenophon (c.430BC-354BC).   Athenian historian. He was a pupil of **Socrates**. He fought as a mercenary soldier for both the Persians and the Spartans, and was banished from Athens as a result. While in exile in Sparta he wrote many books, including *The Anabasis*, about his period with the Persians, and *The Hellenica*, a history of the events of his day. He also wrote about farming, horsemanship and finance, and works on Socrates.

Date chart

This chart lists the most important dates in Ancient Greek history. It also includes some of the events that took place elsewhere in the world during same period; these are shown on indented lines.

Early history

from 40,000BC   The first people settle in Greece, hunting and gathering food.

The Neolithic Period: c.6500-2900BC

c.6500-3000BC   First inhabitants settle on Crete and introduce farming. Pottery is made in Greece and Crete.

    c.6250BC   Çatal Hüyük in Anatolia (modern Turkey) becomes the largest town of its time. Pottery and woollen cloth are manufactured there.

    c.5000BC-4000BC   Farming spreads through Europe.

c.4000BC   Evidence of early inhabitants in the Cyclades, including remains of metalware.

    c.3500BC   The wheel is invented in Sumer in the Middle East.

    c.3200BC   Introduction of pottery in Ecuador, South America.

    c.3100BC   Cities develop in Sumer. Writing develops in Sumer and Egypt.

The Bronze Age: c.2900-1000BC

c.2900BC   Metal is now in widespread use. The population of Greece increases, villages grow into towns and some people become specialized craftsmen.

    c.2686-2181BC   Old Kingdom in Egypt.

    c.2590BC   Pyramid of Cheops is built at Giza in Egypt.

c.2500BC   The city of Troy is founded.

    c.2500BC   Beginning of Indus civilization in India.

c.2100BC   Possible arrival of the first Greek-speaking people in Greece.

c.2000BC   The sail is first used on ships in the Aegean.

    c.2000BC   Building of Stonehenge begins in Britain.

    c.2000BC   Middle kingdom begins in Egypt.

    c.1814BC   First Assyrian Empire begins in the Middle East.

c.1900BC   The first Cretan palaces are built. Rise of Minoan† culture on Crete.

    c.1792-1750BC   Reign of Hammurabi, founder of the Babylonian Empire.

c.1700BC   The Cretan palaces are destroyed by earthquakes, then rebuilt.

c.1600BC   Rise of Mycenaean culture in Greece. The first shaft graves† are built.

    c.1600BC   Towns and cities develop in China.

    c.1567BC   New Kingdom begins in Egypt.

c.1600BC   Tholos† tombs are first used in Greece.

    c.1550BC   Aryans settle in northern India and establish the Hindu religion.

    c.1500BC   Writing in use in China.

c.1500-1450BC   Traditional date given for the eruption of Thera.

c.1450BC   The Cretan palaces are destroyed. The palace at Knossos is taken over by Mycenaeans and rebuilt. Expansion of Mycenaean power and wealth.

c.1400BC   Knossos burns down, and is not rebuilt.

c.1250BC   The main defences are built at Mycenae and other mainland sites. Date traditionally given as the start of the Trojan War.

c.1200BC   Mycenaean power declines and many of their cities are abandoned. Migration of Sea Peoples begins.

    c.1200BC   Jewish religion begins.

    c.1166BC   Death of Ramesses III, last great Egyptian Pharaoh.

    c.1150BC   Olmec civilization begins in Mexico.

The Dark Ages: c.1100-800BC

by 1100BC   The Mycenaean way of life has broken down.

    c.1100BC   Phoenicians spread throughout the Mediterranean, and develop alphabetic writing.

    c.1010-926BC   Kingdom of Israel.

    c.1000BC   Etruscans arrive in Italy.

    c.911BC   New Assyrian Empire begins.

c.900BC   The state of Sparta is founded.

    814BC   Phoenicians found city of Carthage on the North African coast.

The Archaic Period: c.800-500BC

Between 850-750BC   Homer† probably lived at this time.

c.800BC   Greek contact with the other peoples of the Mediterranean resumes. The Greeks adopt the Phoenician style of writing, using it for their own language.

    c.800BC   Aryans move southwards in India.

776BC   First Olympic Games held.

    753BC   Date traditionally given as the founding of the city of Rome.

c.750-650BC   Groups of people start to emigrate from mainland Greece. They found colonies around the Mediterranean.

c.740-720BC   The Spartans begin expanding their territory, and conquer the neighbouring state of Messenia.

    c.700BC   Scythians move into eastern Europe from Asia.

c.650BC   The first tyrants† seize power in Greek mainland states. First coins used in Lydia.

    c.650BC   Iron Age begins in China.

c.630-613BC   The Messenians revolt against the Spartans but are eventually crushed.

    627BC   Neo-Babylonian Empire begins.

621BC   Draco† is appointed *archon*† in Athens and introduces a strict set of laws.

c.594BC   Solon† is appointed *archon* in Athens and begins to reform the political system.

c.550BC   Tyrannies are established in the Greek colonies.

c.550BC   Cyrus II of Persia founds the Persian Empire.

c.546BC   Peisistratus† seizes power as tyrant of Athens.

c.530BC   Beginning of Persian Wars.

by 521BC   King Darius I has expanded Persian Empire from the Nile to the Indus

513BC   The Persians invade Europe.

c.510BC   Monarchy in Rome is replaced by a republic.

508BC   Cleisthenes† seizes power in Athens and introduces reforms which lead to democracy†.

500BC-499BC   The Greek colonies in Ionia revolt against Persian rule.

The Classical Age: c.500-336BC

494BC   The Persians suppress the Ionian revolt.

490BC   The Persians invade the Greek mainland, and are defeated at the Battle of Marathon.

486BC   Death of Siddhartha Gautama, founder of Buddhism.

480BC   Battles of Thermopylae and Salamis.

c.480BC   *The Persians*, the first surviving play by Aeschylus†.

479BC   Battle of Plataea. The Persians are repelled from Greece.

479BC   Death of the Chinese religious teacher Confucius.

478BC   Athens and other Greek states form the Delian League against the Persians.

460-457BC   The Long Walls† are built around Athens and Piraeus. The Acropolis† is rebuilt.

c.450BC   Start of the Celtic culture known as La Tène, named after the site in France where evidence of it was first found.

449BC   The Delian League makes peace with Persia.

445BC   30 Years' Peace declared between Athens and Sparta.

443-429BC   The Age of Pericles†, who is elected *strategos*† every year between these dates.

431-404BC   The Peloponnesian War, fought between Athens and Sparta.

430BC   Athens is hit by plague.

429BC   Death of Pericles.

421BC   50 Years' Peace negotiated by Nicias between Sparta and Athens.

413BC   Athens sends a fleet to Sicily to intervene in a dispute. The fleet is destroyed. War breaks out again between Athens and Sparta.

407BC   Athenian fleet defeated at Notium.

405BC   Athens defeated by Sparta at Battle of Aegospotami.

404BC   Spartan victory over Athens in the Peloponnesian War. The Long Walls are dismantled, the Delian League is dissolved, and Athens is forced to adopt an oligarchic† government, known as the Thirty Tyrants.

403BC   Democracy is reinstated in Athens

399BC   Wars between Sparta and Persia begin. Socrates† is condemned to death.

395-387BC   The Corinthian War. Alliance of Corinth, Athens, Argos and Thebes against Sparta.

394BC   The Persians defeat Sparta at the Battle of Cnidus.

394-391   The Long Walls are rebuilt at Athens.

387BC   Corinthian War ended by the King's Peace, negotiated by the Persians. The Ionian colonies pass to Persian control.

371BC   The Thebans defeat Sparta at the Battle of Leuctra.

362BC   Sparta and Athens defeat Thebes at the Battle of Mantinea.

359BC   Philip II† becomes king of Macedonia.

340BC   Greek states form the Hellenic League against Philip.

338BC   Philip defeats the Hellenic League at the Battle of Chaeronea, and becomes ruler of Greece.

337BC   All Greek states except Sparta form the Corinthian League, led by Philip. The league declares war on Persia.

336BC   Death of Philip. He is succeeded by his son, Alexander†, who becomes leader of the Corinthian League.

335BC   Alexander crushes Thebes.

334BC   Alexander attacks the Persians.

333BC   Alexander defeats the Persians at the Battle of Issus.

332BC   Alexander conquers Phoenicia, Samaria, Judaea, Gaza, and Egypt.

331BC   Sparta joins the Corinthian League. Alexander defeats the Persias at the Battle of Gaugamela.

327BC   Alexander conquers Persia, and advances into India.

323BC   Alexander dies in Babylon.

The Hellenistic Period: c. 323-30BC

323-322BC   The Lamian Wars. The Greek states fight to win independence from the Macedonians, but are defeated.

323-281BC   Wars of the Diadochi† (Alexander's successors).

301BC   Battle of Ipsus. Four rival diadochi kingdoms are set up.

281BC   The Battle of Corupedium ends the Wars of the Diadochi. Three diadochi kingdoms are established: Macedonia (ruled by Antigonas†); Asia Minor (ruled by Seleucus†) and Egypt (ruled by Ptolemy†).

275BC   King Pyrrhus of Epirus is defeated by the Romans in Italy.

266-262BC   The Chremonides War. The Athenians rise against the Antigonids but are suppressed.

221-206BC   Ch'in dynasty in China.

221-179BC   Reign of Philip V of Macedonia.

215BC   Philip V forms an alliance with Hannibal of Carthage, provoking Roman reprisals.

215-205BC   First Macedonian War between Macedonians and Romans.

214BC   Great Wall built in China.

202BC   Philip V forms an alliance with the Seleucid Empire, but Rome intervenes.

202-197BC   Second Macedonian War. Philip V is defeated by the Romans and gives up control of Greece.

179-168BC   Reign of last Macedonian king, Perseus.

171-168BC   Third Macedonian War. The Romans defeat Perseus at the Battle of Pydna. They abolish the Macedonian monarchy and set up four Roman republics.

147-146BC   The Achaean War. The Romans destroy Corinth after a Macedonian Revolt, and impose direct Roman rule on Greece and Macedonia.

Glossary

Many of the Ancient Greek words used in this book are listed and explained in the glossary below. The list also contains some English words that may be unfamiliar. Usually the term given in bold type is the singular. Where the plural is often used, it is given in brackets after the main word.

Acropolis. A fortified city, built on an area of high ground. The word means "high city" in Greek. In Mycenaean times, much of the city was on the acropolis, but later the acropolis was part of a larger city and was often used as a religious sanctuary.

Agora. An open space, in the middle of a Greek city, used for markets and as a meeting place. It was often surrounded by shops and public buildings.

Amphora (amphorae). A large pot with two handles, used to transport and store wine and other liquids.

Andron. A dining room in a private house, used only by the men of the family.

Archon. An Athenian official. The *archons* were very powerful during the Archaic Period, but when democracy was introduced they became less important and retained mainly ceremonial duties.

Aristocrat. A member of a rich, land owning family. The name comes from the Greek word *aristoi*, meaning "the best people".

Attica. Name of the state made up of Athens and the surrounding countryside.

Barbarian. Any foreigner who did not speak Greek. The name came from the strange "bar-bar-bar" noise which the Greeks thought foreigners made when they spoke. It came to mean any uncivilized people.

Black figure ware. A style of pottery decorated with black figures on a red background.

Bronze Age. The period from c.3000-1100BC during which bronze was the most important metal, used for making tools and weapons.

Caryatid. A column carved in the shape of a young woman.

Cella. The main room of a temple, in which the statue of a god or goddess stood.

Chiton. A woman's dress. It was made from a single piece of cloth, fastened at the shoulders.

Chorus. A group of men who took part in plays at the theatre. They all spoke together, often commenting on the action. Sometimes they also sang and danced.

Citizen. A free man who had the right to participate in the government of his city state.

Corinthian column. A style of column whose top is decorated with carved acanthus leaves.

Cuirass. A piece of armour used by hoplite soldiers. It consisted of a breastplate and a backplate joined together by straps.

Cult statue. A statue of the god or goddess which stood in the main room of a temple. People addressed their prayers to the statue.

Democracy. A political system in which all citizens had a say in the government of their state. The word comes from the Greek for "rule by the people".

Diadochi. The name given to the generals who took over the various parts of Alexander the Great's empire after his death. The word means "successors".

Doric column. A plain column with an undecorated top. The *Doric Order* was a style of architecture which used this sort of column.

Electrum. A natural mixture of gold and silver, which was used to make the first coins.

Ephebe. A young Athenian man engaged in two years' compulsory military training.

Faience. Coloured, glazed, earthenware used in Minoan Crete to make decorative objects.

Fresco. A wall painting made by applying paint to wet plaster.

Greave. A piece of armour used by hoplite soldiers. It protected the leg from knee to ankle.

Gymnasium (gymnasia). A sports centre where people could practise athletics. In later years a gymnasium was often a centre of intellectual life too, and might be equipped with a lecture hall and a library.

Gynaeceum. The women's rooms in a private house.

Hellene. The word which the Greeks used to refer to the whole Greek race. It came from the name of a legendary hero, Hellen, who was said to be the father of the Greek people.

Hellenistic age. This term is used to describe the period after the death of Alexander the Great, when Greek language and culture dominated the countries of his former empire.

Herm. A statue of the god Hermes, consisting of a head on a pillar. It usually stood outside the front door of a house and was thought to protect the home.

Hetaira (hetairai). A woman who was specially educated to make conversation, play musical instruments and sing in order to entertain men. *Hetairai* often had love affairs with their clients.

Himation. A type of cloak or scarf, worn by both men and women.

Hoplite. A heavily armed foot soldier who fought in the armies of the Greek city states.

Ionic column. A tall, slender column, whose top was decorated with a swirl called a volute. The *Ionic Order* was a style of architecture which used this sort of column.

Krater. A large vase in which wine was mixed with water.

Labrys. A double headed axe, which was an important sacred symbol in Minoan religion.

Libation. An offering of liquid (wine, milk or blood). It was usually poured over an altar or onto the earth during a religious ceremony.

Linear A. An early form of writing used by the Minoans.

Linear B. An adapted form of Linear A writing, used by the Mycenaeans.

Long Walls. The walls which linked the city of Athens to its port at Piraeus from 460 to 404BC.

Lyre. A stringed musical instrument, made from a tortoise shell and the horns of an ox. Later lyres were made of carved wood.

Megaron. A large hall in a Mycenaean palace, which usually contained four pillars and a hearth. The king conducted state business in the *megaron*.

Metic. A foreign resident living in Athens.

Minoan. The name that the archaeologist Arthur Evans gave to the civilization he discovered on Crete. The term came from the legendary Cretan king, Minos.

Museum. A temple to the Muses (see page 54). The most famous one was built in Alexandria in Egypt during the Hellenistic age. It was a great centre of learning where many scientists and inventors worked.

Mystery Cult. A religion with rituals that were kept very secret. Only people who had been intitiated into the group of worshippers could attend its ceremonies.

Oligarchy. A political system in which a small group of people govern.

Omen. A sign, said to be from the gods, which warned of good or evil to come. Specially trained priests took omens from marks on the livers of sacrificed animals, or from the flight patterns of birds.

Oracle. The word can mean three things: a sacred place where people went to consult a god or goddess; the priest or priestess who spoke on behalf of the deity; or the message from the deity. The most famous oracle was at the Temple of Apollo in Delphi, where a priestess called the Pythia was thought to be able to communicate with the gods.

Ostracism. A special vote held in the Athenian Assembly to banish unpopular politicians. It is so called because the voters scratched the names of people they wanted to expel onto *ostraka*, pieces of broken pottery.

Paidagogos. A special slave who escorted a boy to and from school and supervised him in class.

Patron deity. A god or goddess who was thought to protect a particular place, person or group of people. For example, Athene was the patron goddess of Athens and Hephaestos was the patron god of metal workers.

Peltast. A lightly armed foot soldier, first used by the Thracians and later by the Greek armies.

Peristyle. A row of columns surrounding the outside of a temple.

Phalanx. The formation in which hoplite soldiers fought. It consisted of a block of soldiers, usually eight ranks deep.

Philosopher. The word comes from the Greek for "lover of knowledge". The first philosophers were scholars who studied all aspects of the world around them. Later, however, philosophy became a more specific subject. Philosophers began trying to understand the purpose of the universe and the nature of human life and behaviour.

Pithos (pithoi). A large, earthenware storage jar used in Minoan Crete.

Polis. An independent Greek state, consisting of a city and the surrounding countryside.

Pythia. The priestess who spoke on behalf of the god Apollo at the oracle of Delphi.

Red figure ware. A style of pottery decorated with red figures on a black background.

Relief. A sculpture carved on a flat slab of stone. The stone was carved away so that the picture stood out against a flat background.

Rhapsode. A man who made his living by reciting poetry at religious festivals or private parties.

Rhyton. A special pot, in the shape of a horn or an animal's head, with a hole pierced in the lower end to act as a spout. It was often used in religious ceremonies to make a libation.

Sarcophagus. A stone coffin.

Shaft grave. An early form of Mycenaean tomb, in which the body was buried at the bottom of a deep shaft.

Soothsayer. Someone who was thought to be able to foresee the future.

Stele (stelae). A stone slab used to mark a grave.

Stoa. A long, roofed passageway with columns on one which provided shelter from the sun, wind and rain. The *stoa* was found in town centres, where it often formed the side of an *agora* and sometimes contained shops or offices. Some religious sanctuaries also had a *stoa*.

Strategos (strategoi). An Athenian army commander. There were ten *strategoi*, who were elected annually. Under the democratic system, the *strategoi* also had the power to implement the policies which were decided by the Council and the Assembly.

Terracotta. A mixture of unfired clay, sand, and particles of clay that has already been baked. It was used to make tiles, and for small statues, which are sometimes called terracottas.

Tholos. A type of Mycenaean grave, consisting of a beehive-shaped room entered through a long corridor. Later the name was also given to circular buildings with conical roofs. These often had pillars round the outside.

Trireme. A warship with three rows of oars.

Tyrant. A Greek word for "ruler". A tyrant was someone who governed with absolute power. In the Archaic Period many Greek states were governed by tyrants. Later the word came to mean any cruel, oppressive ruler.

Index

First published in 1990 by Usborne Publishing Ltd.
83–85 Saffron Hill, London EC1N 8RT, England.